THE SORCERESS

AND THE

SKULL

THE SORCERESS

AND THE

SKULL

BY

DONALD MICHAEL PLATT

The Sorceress and the Skull
By Donald Michael Platt
Copyright © 2016 Donald Michael Platt

ISBN-13: 978-1-942756-56-9(Paperback)
ISBN :-978-1-942756-57-6 (e-book)

BISAC Subject Headings:
FIC024000 FICTION / Occult
FIC030000 FICTION / Suspense
FIC039000 FICTION / Visionary & Metaphysical

Cover Illustration by Christine Horner

Address all correspondence to:

Penmore Press LLC
920 N Javelina Pl
Tucson AZ 85748

INVOCATION OF THE LAW AGAINST INEPT CRITICS

Who reads this verse consider it thoughtfully.
Let the profane and ignorant not be tempted;
All: Astrologers, Simpletons, and Barbarians avoid this;
Who does otherwise, may he be cursed according to
    sacred rite.

                    Nostradamus VI:100

TO THE READER

The author neither endorses nor rejects the possibility that Nostradamus could foresee the future.

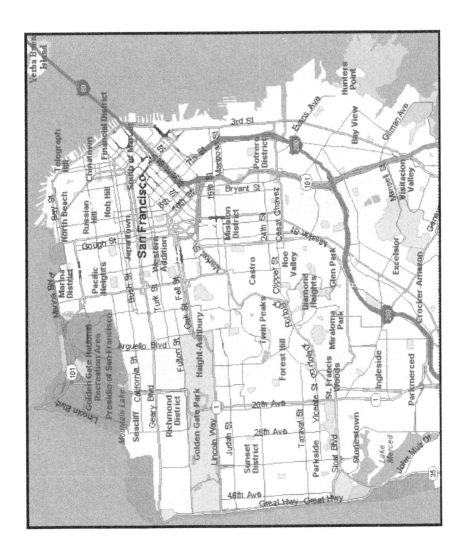

The best way to predict the future is to invent it.
Alan Kay, conceiver of the laptop computer

PART I

THOSE PREDICTED TO CONVERGE

CHAPTER 1
OF ANCIENT BLOOD

Dr. César Dastiel hurried on foot through the dark Provençal countryside, immortalized by Impressionists and Fauvists in more hospitable seasons. He crossed an untilled field by a deserted farmhouse and ramshackle barn and went into the woods beyond. At a specific location, Dastiel scooped away soil until he found the handle of a trap door. He twisted it left and right until he heard a click. Dastiel lifted the door and descended into an ancient catacomb known only to the firstborns of his family. Moving through a maze of turns and forks, he counted stones along a wall and pressed against one of them, which opened a section of its facade. Dastiel entered a spacious vault and made the necessary preparations.

Hours later, he awakened from a self-induced trance; he was seated at a table where a flickering candle flame illuminated a brass bowl filled with water and laurel branches balancing on a nearby tripod giving him enough light to read his notebook. There it was: no mistaking it.

THE SORCERESS AND THE SKULL

Automatic writing confirmed the horoscope he had cast for his daughter, born eleven hours ago in St. Rémy at twelve noon, 14 December, according to the Julian calendar, 21 December. according to Gregorian reckoning.

Dastiel left the table and lit three tapers on a silver-filigreed candelabrum. Gold embossed Christian names glistened on the spines of rich burgundy leather-bound volumes filling shelves along the walls from floor to ceiling. They contained prophecies for each member of his family, all who had lived before him; others, unnamed, for those yet to be born. The largest untitled tome lay to the right against the one bearing his own name, CÉSAR IX, and he carried it to the table. With unsullied white gloves, he reverently lifted the cover and read each word of every page written centuries ago.

Dastiel had been born with many of his family's well-developed gifts of foresight, but he lacked the ability to interpret with precise accuracy all these ambiguous prophecies. Yet he understood this much: the charts he had cast revealed his daughter to be the Predicted One, the first in five hundred years blessed with The Understanding equal to if not greater than the Great Oracle himself. Had she not been born on the same month, day, and instant in the same city as He Who Saw and Understood the Future? Although his daughter might have flashes of precognition from first consciousness; her genius would manifest itself after she entered puberty. No one except his wife-cousin Anne and his two sisters, who had helped deliver this child, must be aware of her existence. They were the last surviving descendants of the Great Seer. Powerful enemies who coveted these unpublished prophecies had come close, in their determination to acquire them, to exterminating his family. They would want his daughter as well.

2

During his wife's pregnancy, Dastiel had made every possible arrangement to protect his child: false identities and necessary passports, Swiss bank accounts and trusts, and residences established throughout the world. He would have to do more.

Dastiel returned to the shelves, removed a black velvet pouch, and uncovered a fearsome malachite chimera with eyes of gold. He spoke to the foot-high sculpture as if it were capable of thought and action: "Goji, you must do all in your power to safeguard my daughter."

Golden eyes reflected light from the candles, convincing Dastiel it understood. He next opened an ancient terracotta jar and applied gold leaf to the burgundy leather. His daughter would have many pseudonyms, yet one true name. He wrote, first on the spine, MICHELE VII, and then on the cover, MICHELE DE NOSTREDAME.

***

Dastiel brooded at his desk in the study of a nineteenth-century manse he owned in St. Remy de Province.

Terrible times loomed on the horizon. He and Anne might not survive to guide their daughter into adulthood. That much Dastiel could foresee. Of his two sisters, reliable twenty-four-year-old Madeleine had some of their family's gifts of precognition. Eighteen-year-old Catherine, a brilliant student at the Sorbonne and a stunning beauty, presented a conundrum. Secretive, she envied her brother for his ability to cast accurate horoscopes and sister for her episodes of clairvoyance. How might she react to his Michele?

Dastiel removed a folder from his desk drawer. It contained the recent horoscope he had created for his youngest sister and confirmed what he feared most.

Catherine could not be trusted and presented a danger to his newborn daughter. The golden eyes of the chimera on his desk flashed agreement with his assessment. Its malachite veins pulsated.

Dastiel returned to Anne, who slept, exhausted from a difficult birth. Madeleine cooed to the newborn, and Catherine held her crying, restless niece as if she were a valuable possession. César took his daughter away from Catherine and placed her in bed beside Anne. Michele stopped crying, no longer agitated. He told his sisters to leave and locked the bedroom door.

The following morning, before sunrise, Madeleine knocked on the bedroom door until César awakened. Distraught, she urged him to come with her to Catherine's room where an armoire and drawers had been emptied. César went to a window overlooking the driveway. His Citroen was parked where he had left it. Downstairs in the study, he stood in front of an open wall safe. Copies of Nostradamus' unpublished quatrains were missing. César gave Madeleine the keys to his car.

"You know what you must do."

A week later, César and Anne listened to Madeleine describe what she learned in Paris. Catherine never returned to her apartment or classes at the Sorbonne. She also closed her bank account.

César understood Catherine's motives and anticipated her subsequent moves. "We must leave St. Rémy now."

CHAPTER 2
SWITZERLAND

In late August of 1939, Madeleine Picard awakened from a brief trance at the breakfast table in the family chalet outside Mollens, Switzerland. She stepped outside onto a wraparound balcony and breathed the crisp early morning air to help clear her head.

Set in a bucolic hamlet amidst forests and pastures at 1,070 meters, the chalet faced a green grazing field where cows ruminated. At the far end lay a small cluster of homes dominated by a church spire, suggesting a picture postcard cliché. Mollens, with its friendly population of a few hundred and relative obscurity, had provided a sanctuary for her family after they left France.

The time had come to leave Switzerland and all of Europe. That was why César and Anne had gone to visit their banks and attorney in Geneva, a 180-kilometer drive from Mollens. The plan had been for Madeleine and Michele to join them tomorrow.

She lit a *Galois* and recalled the vision during her trance.

5

César and Anne lay naked side by side on tables in a morgue, their bodies almost unrecognizable because of severe burns. What sinister force had prevented César from foreseeing their deaths? How best to tell Michele?

"The Byzantine."

Madeleine had not seen Michele join her on the balcony. "You dreamed and saw your parents?"

'Yes. They are dead."

"Michele, our visas and passports are current. We leave for Geneva, and from there fly to French Canada, Quebec."

***

Earthquakes.

Floods.

Fire from the skies.

Strange vehicles and weapons.

Faces briefly appearing.

Past, present, and future. All at once.

None making any sense, yet she divined the presence of so many who intended to harm her, and one she sensed but could not see who would protect her.

From whom? From what?

***

In a hotel near Genève Aéroport, Madeleine left her sofa bed, switched on the lamp atop a nightstand by Michele and waited for her niece to stop thrashing in bed. She had not mourned during her parents' cremations, nor did she want their ashes kept in an urn.

César and Anne had died among a dozen others during a

fire at their hotel, severe burns and smoke inhalation certified as the cause of death.

Michele awakened. "I saw a new person in my dreams, a tall man. He placed a cloak around my shoulders as if to shield me."

"He is mentioned often in the prophecies as *Le Crâne* and is destined to protect you."

CHAPTER 3
LE CRÂNE

Except for hordes of servicemen in uniform on passes enjoying the City's offerings in 1944, San Francisco seemed unchanged to Marco Antonio Dante, but his personal life and physical appearance had been altered forever. Earlier in the day, Dante had been released from Letterman Army Hospital near the Presidio with an honorable discharge, and he anticipated tactless reactions to his reconstructed skin-taut face. Two restaurants refused him service. On sidewalks, strangers gaped horrified, looked away and covered their children's eyes; or they stared at Dante with expressions of pity. Two hundred and five pounds on a six-foot-three inch frame, if he smiled, his skull-like face added an aura of menace.

The day after the Japanese attacked Pearl Harbor, December 8, 1941, Dante had enlisted in the Army. Three months later and commissioned second Lieutenant, he returned to the City to attend the funerals of his parents, younger brother, and sister, who died in a head-on along a tule fogbound stretch of the Bayshore Highway south of San Francisco. On their way home from a cousin's wedding in San Mateo, a drunk driver smashed into their car. After the burials, Dante fought in Sicily and Italy until wounded. Hospitalized in England, he recovered from burns, skin grafts, and injuries that ripped away thumb and forefinger joints from his left hand. Moved to Letterman Army Hospital in the City, Dante endured a final surgery and a thorough psychiatric evaluation to help him adjust to his new unrecognizable, mutilated face.

***

Dante was unable to relax in his Edwardian three-story brownstone home in Pacific Heights on Buchanan Street near the corner of Green Street. Too many memories and possessions of his parents and siblings unsettled him. He considered selling the place and moving elsewhere. Insurance settlements and a substantial inheritance had made Dante a man of independent means.

That evening, Dante walked the misty streets of San Francisco, listening to the familiar clanging of cable cars traversing the hills and lugubrious foghorns sounding from the Bay. Moisture from the mist collected on his Fedora and beige Raglan tweed overcoat as he ambled toward *Shanty Malone's* on Sacramento around the corner of Montgomery in the City's financial district, where he had arranged to meet his best friend from their grade school and college days. No unescorted women were allowed in barn-like *Shanty's*, one of the great last saloons. At the bar, a president of a bank or department store might argue with a longshoreman about who was the eighth-ranked middleweight boxer in 1928. Alumni from rival universities often set chairs on the floor for missing teammates and ran football plays in the middle of the saloon. Late night brawls were common.

Drinking at the bar, Beefy Irish-Armenian Doyle Conlon had started as right tackle next to Dante's end position for the Lowell High School and Cal football teams. Conlon tried to enlist in the Army with Dante the day after the Pearl Harbor attack, but a perforated eardrum and a bad knee from football injuries classified him as 4-F. Rejected by the armed forces, Doyle followed his father into SFPD. Captain Conlon, Chief Dullea and D.A. Edmund "Pat" Brown also graduated from Lowell. Able and favored, Doyle was now Inspector Sergeant Conlon.

Three years had passed since they had last seen each other. Dante hung his hat and Raglan on a coat pole, prepared himself for a typical reaction of horror or pity to his altered face, and sat in the empty chair to Conlon's right.

"So, what's new, Doyle?"

Conlon stared at Dante. "Who the hell are ... Jesus, Marco, It's really you, When did they let you out of Letterman? I tried to see you there, but you'd just had an operation. You were still unconscious from the anesthetics, and your face was wrapped in bandages."

"That was my last operation. They released me this morning with an honorable discharge. I saw my father's partners this afternoon to settle personal matters, and here I am. As you can see, my face got chewed a bit." Dante showed Conlon his damaged hand. "And I might rival Django Reinhardt for the title of best three-fingered guitarist in the world... if I knew how to play the damn thing."

"But you're okay otherwise?"

"Mentally, yes, if that's what you're asking."

"Good attitude." Conlon ordered a round of drinks, and they touched glasses. "Welcome home, Marco. Going back to

Law School, or is it too early to ask?"

"No. I studied Law because my father expected me to join his firm."

"Terrible thing that happened to your family."

Dante's grunt terminated that thread of conversation, and Conlon changed the subject. "Have you seen your fiancée Carole yet?"

"She Dear Johned me to my face."

"I didn't know. I won't ask why. At least you weren't married. If you're not returning to Law School, what will you do?"

"Paint."

"Houses?"

"Art."

"Really? I don't remember ever seeing you at any easel. You any good?"

"It began as therapy in England. Am I good, you ask? Let the public judge. Sold all the paintings I did at the hospitals. Might take some classes at the San Francisco Art Institute."

Dante did not want to talk about his combat experiences. "How's the crime business?"

"Mostly light stuff. Intra-service brawls, which the MPs and SPs deal with. The usual B-Girl antics in the Tenderloin District, and an occasional crime of passion." Conlon finished his scotch, encouraged Dante to do the same, and ordered another round. "Any plans for the night?"

"No."

"Then we have to celebrate your return. Mind if I ask? Is your plumbing in working order?"

"So they told me. I haven't had any opportunity to confirm it since I was hospitalized."

"Then let me treat you to a couple of hours at Sally Stanford's."

THE SORCERESS AND THE SKULL

Dante had never experienced delights offered by the most famous and expensive brothel in the City. "Is she still paying off politicians and SFPD?"

Conlon grinned. "Why, Marco, that would be corruption."

"I'll pass on your offer, Doyle. I'll drink here until I've had enough."

"Then I'll keep you company."

**

Dante walked home through a dense fog and sensed someone followed. Yet, each time he slowed and looked back, he saw and heard nothing suspicious. Eyes and ears on full alert, he hesitated at the front steps of his house. A persistent meowing came from the front door. Dante went to the burnt sienna, yellow-eyed cat sitting still on its haunches stiff as a sentinel. It reminded him of Egyptian cat-goddess statuettes.

Dante bent and petted the cat, which rewarded him with relentless purring. The cat arched its back under his hand, and he discovered its gender was female. "Cat, I can use some company, so whoever you are, you may stay the night, or longer if you wish."

Dante opened the door, and the cat rushed inside ahead of him as if she knew where to go. He switched on the lights, grateful his father's partners had notified PG&E and the telephone company to connect their services. Dante next went into the library, where the cat observed him from the mantle above the cold fireplace.

"If you intend to stay, I must give you a name. No idea what you were called before."

Dante found a volume from a 1944 *Britannica* set and opened the encyclopedia's section on Egyptian gods and goddesses. The cat made a noise, not quite a meow, but something that sounded more like *mee-ay*, and Dante saw a name belonging to one of the cat goddesses.

"You say your name is Mié? Then Mié it shall be."

Dante went to another volume and learned Mié was of the Abyssinian breed. "Lucky for you I did some marketing today. I have no cat food or litter box, but let's go into the kitchen, and I'll give you a can of tuna and a bowl of water. Tomorrow, we will find a vet so I can learn more about you. I hope you'll stay. This house is too big for one person."

Dante placed a bowl of water and can of tuna on the floor. He watched Mié eat and drink. Had she followed him from *Shanty's*? Why did he sense the Abyssinian had come into his life for a specific reason?

CHAPTER 4
THE CITY

It was January, 1946. Michele awakened in the darkness of a chilly and damp San Francisco winter night and left her bed. In the hallway, a sliver of light at the bottom of a door indicated Aunt Madeleine was not yet asleep. Michele knocked, entered, and stood over her aunt, who put aside the book she had been reading.

"Another dream, Michele?"

"Yes."

"Do you wish to tell me about it?"

This time Michele spoke about her dream. "There was a man whose face resembled a skull, terribly disfigured, but he had kind eyes. I liked him."

"*Le Crâne*. Did you see more?"

"There was another, a beautiful blonde woman, but not a real person. It was a painting, a portrait, and in it she was surrounded by ice."

"*La Blond d'Hiver*. The Winter Blonde."

"You never told me about her, Aunt Madeleine. Is she a real person?"

"Yes, she was mentioned in the quatrains your Aunt Catherine stole. It is encouraging that you dreamed of *La Blond d'Hiver*."

"Why?"

"It has been late in coming, but the day you become a woman is near. Then, you shall have The Understanding. For the first time, I can tell you this. Your powers will be beyond those of any other human who lives, has lived, and shall be born. Your ancient blood will speak to you. Then you shall know what your powers are and how best to use those amazing gifts."

"You always speak of The Understanding, but you never tell me what it is."

"You have already experienced some of it in your dreams. You shall know everything when you have all powers of precognition and more, so much more."

"But what are they, Aunt Madeleine?"

"You have seen the one who has been predicted to safeguard you. Although I lack all the gifts you shall have one day, I am using those I do have to find *Le Crâne* before it is too late. That is why we left Quebec and moved here to San Francisco."

"And the blonde lady?"

"I do not yet know her role in your future."

"There are others I have seen in dreams. Who are they?"

"One is our greatest adversary, named *Verbedieu* in the prophecies, also known as 'The Byzantine'. The others are that monster's evil minions. Our nemeses are near, closer than they have ever been, but in the end, they shall not harm you."

"Has that been foretold as well?"

"Yes." Madeleine left her bed and walked Michele back to her room. She knew better than to tuck her niece under the covers and attempt to kiss the girl goodnight. "I believe my sister Catherine is seeking you. For good or for ill, I cannot say. Go back to sleep now, my child. I have much work to do."

***

Michele completed her morning ablutions and put a robe over her pajamas. She went downstairs to the kitchen and carried a tray containing coffee and croissants into the drape-shrouded library. It was Michele's favorite room. Laid out the same wherever they lived, its furnishings, rugs, books, and bric-a-brac had been with their family throughout the centuries, so her aunt often said.

Madeleine sat in a trance at an ebony desk by candle light chanting in French until she became aware of Michele's presence.

"I disturbed you, Aunt Madeleine."

"No, it is all right." She waited until Michele sat in one of the comfortable floral upholstered armchairs opposite the desk. "I too have seen *Le Crâne* for the first time, Michele. I believe I know where to find him. It must be soon, for a dark, shadowy figure approaches."

Michele sat forward. "Tell me more, Aunt Madeleine."

"It was a presence, a chill that froze my heart, nothing specific."

"But Aunt Madeleine, you have said the prophecies were meant to warn us, and if we heed them, we can survive whatever our nemeses try to do to us."

"Of course they are warnings. Although the stars impel, they do not compel. In the end, we can choose our destinies. Yet, some things that happen to us are inevitable."

"Of what use is it to know the future when you cannot change it?"

Madeleine did not reply.

"Perhaps you are wrong and misinterpreted the shadowy figure."

"It may not be awful as you have been imagining. My end shall be your beginning, so the prophecies have shown me. That is why it was necessary for me to bring you to San Francisco and find *La Blond d'Hiver* and *Le Crâne*. Our battle against a great evil is about to begin."

"I wish I could be normal, like everyone else."

Madeleine sighed. "I, too, had those same desires when I was your age. That is why I want you to live as an ordinary thirteen-year old girl and attend a school here in San Francisco."

Madeleine inserted the prophecies in an oversized envelope and placed it in a desk drawer. "I have said more than I should, Michele. Now, I must dress and leave on important business. Tomorrow we shall be meeting with the Principal at your new school."

***

Left alone in the library, Michele stroked a malachite chimera on the desk. It had appeared one day in this room, and other times at night on her bedroom dresser. Aunt Madeleine never explained where it came from, or how an inanimate figure moved from room to room. For some reason Michele could not explain, she had given the chimera a medieval name.

"Goji, if you can see into the immediate future, tell me: who or what is the dark shadowy figure my aunt described?"

The chimera's veins appeared about to burst, and its eyes glowed. Michele heard and understood a voice speaking an unfamiliar language. Something else occurred. Confidence replaced fear.

"Thank you, Goji. Now I have the courage to face *Vebedieu*, The Byzantine, whomsoever he may be."

CHAPTER 5
SEEKING MICHELE

The Woman told her servants she did not want to be disturbed. Wearing a black hooded velour robe, she reclined on a divan in her bedroom suite at a Turkish palace built on the edge of a promontory with a panoramic view of the Bosporus and the Black Sea. The raging waters below were never so dark, illuminated by frequent lightning, which caused a power outage. Candles on sconces and candelabras flickered from the wailing wind whistling through window edges.

The vile weather outside and The Woman's mood were one, as if she had conjured a storm to match her fury. She dwelled upon her one great mistake. She had financed the losing side, sat out the last year of the war in neutral Turkey, and now suffered through one of the worst winters of her lifetime.

The Woman selected a Havana from a side table, sniffed and rolled it close to her ear. Satisfied, she clipped an end, lit and savored the cigar. She poured aged cognac from a bottle beside the humidor and opened a folder. The Woman withdrew and read copies of valuable quatrains written almost five hundred years earlier that predicted her existence. She had stolen and murdered to obtain them.

The Woman focused on her main goal about to be achieved, according to her interpretation of the prophecies: Find and possess the elusive girl identified in those quatrains to have more powers of precognition than any human living, dead, or to be born. Unlimited wealth and political influence were not enough to satisfy. The Woman desired omniscience.

Black night, black of heart, The Woman reviewed strategies and tactics she believed would ensure a successful outcome. She looked forward to her flight tomorrow, a return to warm California and a more comfortable estate, down the Peninsula from San Francisco where the climax had been predicted to take place.

CHAPTER 6
HIGH SCHOOL REGISTRATION

Michele and her aunt, who went by the name of Mrs. Desaix, sat in Principal LeRoy Stephens' office at Lowell High School, situated on Hayes between Ashbury and Masonic. Mr. Stephens had a kind face. The woman he introduced as Michele's counselor, Miss Pugmire, a lean spinster, had a more austere manner.

Stephens finished reading Michele's academic records, passed them to Miss Pugmire, and said, "Mrs. Desaix, you were fortunate to find shelter in Canada during the war and provide so fine an education for your niece. I believe Michele belongs in our high school for the current semester, which offers the best academic education in the State of California, if not the entire USA. The problem is her young age and advanced mind. I recommend she transfer to a university in the fall."

"Yes, that is what her educators advised in Canada. I prefer that my niece attend a university in the fall. By then she will have become better acclimated to your American ways of teaching."

"In the meantime, I cannot place Michele in freshman classes."

"Freshman?"

"First-year student. Michele is thirteen, but given her high I.Q, which is almost off the scale, and the courses she passed in Canada, I shall place Michele in a ninth grade freshman homeroom, to be with students close to her age. Some are a year ahead, which is not unusual at Lowell, but we will allow her to take classes at higher academic levels."

Miss Pugmire took over. "Mrs. Desaix, we will pre-enroll Michele in each course and assign someone from the Scroll, our girls' honor society, to show your niece around the school. The spring semester begins a week from today, Monday, February 4th." Pugmire handed Michele a sheet of paper. "Here are your classes, room numbers, times of day, and teachers' names."

Michele read her schedule that began at 8 AM in a fifteen-minute homeroom,

Miss Pugmire continued, "10th Grade English will help you become familiar with American vocabulary, spelling, and Literature. You are fluent in French, German, Italian, and have completed advanced courses in Latin and Greek, which is why you will take Spanish. PE, Physical Education, is required by the State of California. You also have Calculus, United States History, and Advanced Composition. One more thing, here is the key for your hall locker."

Miss Pugmire rose, opened the door, and beckoned an older girl Michele thought attractive. She wore a white blouse under a red cardigan sweater with a big white L on the side and three white stripes on the upper arms. A red and white cap topped her blonde hair.

"Barbara, this is Mrs. Desaix and her niece Michele,

whom we have enrolled. Michele, Mrs. Desaix, Barbara Boswell is a senior and president of the Scroll."

"Everyone calls me Babs."

"We have assigned Michele her classes, and we would like you to show her around the school."

Madeleine stayed to confer with Principal Stephens and Miss Pugmire, and Michele stepped into the hall with Babs Boswell. "It is so quiet here."

"Everyone is taking their final exams. I've finished mine."

Babs familiarized Michele with Lowell's layout and wrote a list of necessities for the first day of school: a binder to hold pens, pencils, ruler and spiral notebooks; a combination lock for her gym locker; and something oddly named a Pee-Chee used to hold loose-leaf papers, stationary, returned tests and reports. She told Michele that Mehde's Drugstore, kitty-corner from Lowell on Hayes and Ashbury, sold textbook covers. Boys could leave the campus during lunch, but not the girls, because the school was too close to the wooded Golden Gate Park Panhandle. She gave Michele a small white brochure with a big red L on the cover.

"This contains more information for new students."

"Babs, are you wearing a special school sweater?"

"No, it's my boyfriend's. He's on the football team." Babs scrutinized Michele's open Navy blue overcoat, plain beige woolen crewneck sweater, and gray skirt. "Before we return to the Principal's office, I want to tell you how most of the girls dress here at Lowell."

***

Michele and Madeleine spent the afternoon shopping for a school wardrobe suggested by Babs Boswell: pullover and cardigan cashmere sweaters, assorted skirts that fell well below the knee some pleated, blouses, bobby sox, saddle shoes and penny loafers. They also purchased babushka scarves popular with the high school girls as protection against the City's strong winds that chapped skin and burned ears.

Michele felt big city energy emanating along the crowded streets, from Roos Brothers at Stockton and Market to the elegant department stores by Union Square: *I Magnin, Joseph Magnin, The White House*, and *The City of Paris*, which she liked best because of its French café in the basement.

Darkness came early in January, and they were eager to hurry home. Tomorrow Michele would shop for her basic school supplies.

"Aunt Madeleine, going to a school with boys will be a new experience for me."

"Ignore them."

"Aunt Madeleine, we are being followed."

***

The Woman considered her next move. One of her agents reported seeing Michele and her aunt. Unfortunately, the fool lost them in traffic and failed to learn where they resided.

Unless Michele was schooled at home, she would be attending school. Eight were public, two were Catholic schools for boys, two were Catholic schools for girls, and two private schools were for girls from the best families. All were on what was called the semester system. The new semester began on the first Monday in February. Michele's home address should be easy to find among files in the school administrative office for new enrollees.

The Woman smiled a hard, cold smile.

CHAPTER 7
RISING DARK

A month into her first semester at Lowell, Michele looked forward each day to attending school. She thought the courses easy, her classmates intelligent and academically motivated, excepting bright underachievers.

Michele became aware of one girl who resented her for an academic reason. Their calculus teacher, an elderly man in his final semester before retiring, graded his classes harshly. One could average 95 and earn a B if three students had higher numbers. Joy McClellan had earned an A the previous semester, but now received B's on her weekly tests because Michele, whom she regarded as both threat and interloper, scored 100 each time.

Joy began to harass Michele on campus: tripping, bumps, a hand reaching from behind to pull books or binder from her arms, and relentless glares in the classroom. The last Friday in February, their teacher gave Joy another B on an exam, and at the end of school, a shove down the stairs caused Michele to fall hard at the bottom.

***

On the way home, Michele sensed someone following. She waited at the last moment to step onto a nearby streetcar and evade whomsoever he might be. Aside from Joy McClellan, that was another concern she must deal with. When Michele arrived home, Madeleine was preparing their daily 4:30 PM traditional *Goûter*, a demitasse of coffee instead of tea, and a biscuit with blueberry preserves.

After a quick hello to her aunt, Michele hurried upstairs and tended to scrapes and bruises before going into her own library adjacent to the bedroom. She sat in a Gothic high back chair at an ebony desk by a brass bowl atop a tripod. Michele pulled closer to her a journal covered by a strange fabric similar to jute, with vivid stripes of deep orange and light blue. It lay open to unsullied pages.

Michele dipped the sharp point of a crow's feather quill in an inkwell and thought about the major incidents of her day until she entered a trance and wrote in glyphs millennia older than the pyramids. Goji stood watching beside Michele's writing hand.

***

Close to midnight, Dante had a visitor. Conlon looked ill and disheveled. "I need a drink, Marco."

Dante invited Conlon into the den and gestured toward the bar. "Help yourself. You look like hell. What's going on, Doyle?"

Conlon poured and drank a double scotch. He refilled his glass and slumped in an armchair. Mié rubbed against his legs and leaped onto an arm of the chair, listening with interest.

THE SORCERESS AND THE SKULL

"Marco, it was the seventeen year old daughter of shipping magnate Cecil McClellan. The most nauseating crime scene I've seen. Even the guys from Emergency barfed. A maid found Joy McClellan alive in her bedroom. Someone lacerated the girl's face beyond recognition, left her eyes untouched. No sign of forced entry, and ...."

Dante let Conlon vent. He had his own problems. Something inexplicable had begun to affect his ability to paint, and now an unsettling foreboding infused the room.

***

First Saturday evening in March, Associate Professor Sandrine Arnoul, Ph.D.'s in Linguistics, Classical Languages, French Literature and History, and fluent in more than a dozen other languages, closed the last page of her marked galley proof for presentation on Monday morning to the University of California Press for publication. Sandrine locked the galley in a desk drawer. She had decorated her small office to make it homey. Ferns and elephant ear plants greened the corners. A bookcase dominated most of the wall to her left, with a quality print of *Mask Still Life III* by the Expressionist Emil Nolde above. A file cabinet, small Frigidaire, and a reproduction of Edward Middleton's haunting *Adagio* filled the right. A burnt orange rug she had woven herself covered the floor from entry to a mahogany desk in front of the window.

Sandrine went to the Frigidaire and opened a bottle of *Veuve Cliquot* she had saved for this special occasion, the completion of a book that had consumed all her waking and much of her sleeping moments for more than two years: *The Bridge Between French Medieval and Classical Poetry from Christine de Pisan and François Villon to the Poets of the*

DONALD MICHAEL PLATT

Seventeenth Century.

She popped the cork and poured champagne into her coffee mug. The phosphorescent numbers and hands of the clock on her desk glowed 11:58 PM, Saturday. The time and day did not surprise Sandrine. She had worked many overnighters and weekenders here in her office. Now it was over.

Sandrine drank champagne and speculated about her career. Because the Comparative Literature Department Committee approved the book, she expected a promotion from Assistant to Full Professor with rights of tenure, provided the Department Dean kept his promise. No reason for him not to.

Sandrine had received offers to teach at several Ivies and Stanford, but something she could not articulate at that time impelled her to choose U.C. Berkeley. Was it the champagne, exhaustion, or both? Sandrine had trouble focusing. Her eyelids felt as if they were lifting concrete blocks, and she fell asleep at the desk.

The Gargoyle often makes his perch
On a cathedral or a church,
Where, mid-ecclesiastic style,
He smiles an early Gothic smile.
Humorist Oliver Herford:

PART II
FIRST WEEK IN MARCH,
1946

CHAPTER 8
BIZARRE MONDAY MORNING

It was 1 AM when Dante threw another charcoal drawing against the third floor studio wall. The violent action startled Mié, the burnt sienna six-year-old Abyssinian perched like a miniature Sphinx atop the burgundy leather couch he used for naps between long sessions at his easel. Why the stray had adopted him was something only the cat knew.

He stared at the drawing. The situation had become ridiculous, irrational too. Some mysterious force controlled his hand and compelled him to draw a woman he had never met or seen before. This had been going on for three days. These drawings resembled Holbein in style, nothing like his heavy impasto Impressionist paintings of the City and Bay that sold well at *The Anxious Asp*, a popular North Beach venue for jazz combos, folk singers, and rising comics.

There had to be a logical explanation and a simple remedy to end it, yet Dante could not prevent the unwanted specter from haunting his canvases. He returned to the easel, watched over by Mié, his severest critic. Dante saw the

31

Abyssinian staring at the drawings. He looked into the cat's yellow eyes for an answer and stroked her shiny coat.

"Well, Mié, can your ancient cat-goddess wisdom and reliable feline intuition tell me what the hell is going on?"

Mié responded with a bell-like meow, punctuated with a question mark and faced the window. So did Dante. He should have been able to see the Bay, Alcatraz, and the Golden Gate Bridge, but a dense fog obscured everything.

Mié leaped to the windowsill. She stood on her hind legs, scratched at the glass, and purred. Dante followed, and for an instant, the mist dissolved. He blinked to be sure he was not seeing things. Was that some mythical gargoyle drenched in blood hovering opposite Mié? It disappeared, enveloped by the fog, and the Abyssinian returned to the comfort of her cat tree.

The hospital shrink at Letterman had warned Dante about flashbacks, but there were no bloody gargoyles flying in the battle zones. Could it have been the scotch? Unlikely. He had not imbibed enough to feel a buzz.

Dante checked the time. Past midnight. Neither sleepy nor physically tired, something compelled him to sketch anew on an unsullied canvas.

A half hour later, Dante stared yet again in dismay at what he had done. The drawing was identical to the last one, to each one of them, as if part of a signed and numbered series of graphics. Beneath a chignon, the woman's features were subordinate to large brown eyes, haunted and despairing, as if begging him for help. Hell, he was the one who needed help.

***

Dante opened his front door. "Jesus, Doyle, it's almost

two AM and you look like death warmed over."

"I saw the light in your studio and knew you were still awake. If you'd seen what I saw, Marco ... I need a scotch and don't want to drink alone."

Dante brought Conlon into the studio and poured him a double. "What happened, Doyle?"

"About 8 PM we got a call about a victim in the Heights. He was mutilated as if some wild animal had shredded him. Sickened everyone. Still awaiting the autopsy report. If the press learns about it, they will terrify the City."

"You said it was here in the Heights?"

"A few blocks from you, and a block from the McClellans. The victim could not have seen what hit him in the thick soup out there. Definitely not a robbery. Remember what I told you about the McClellan girl? It's the same M.O. I can't begin to guess what kind of creature is capable of doing that kind of damage."

Dante chose not to tell Conlon about the bloodstained apparition in the window.

***

Later that morning, Dante scowled at another drawing. Same face, same woman. To clear his head, he went to the bay window in the third-floor studio, drank black coffee, and took in the clear view of the Marina below, Alcatraz, the Golden Gate Bridge, and Sausalito-Tiburon beyond. Next, Dante went to the bathroom and debated whether to shave or not. He had tried to grow a beard Because of the damage to his face a few pathetic, wispy clusters of hair grew here and there.

One moment Dante was shaving his face smooth before the mirror; the next thing he knew, he was in Dwinelle Hall, at the University of California in the outer office of Dr. Nelson Warwick, Dean of Comparative Literature. Dante did not recognize the cherry blonde receptionist until he read the nameplate on her desk that read Cheryl Hale. Miss Hale had been a fixture in the office before the war. Cosmetic surgery had restructured her face to artificial perfection.

Miss Hale remembered Dante. In the midst of their conversation, a stunning woman entered the office. Wearing a forest-green woolen dress, she was not a typical California tanned but a winter blonde with lacquered pale complexion, her hair tied in a severe French bun. Oversized dark amber-tinted glasses obscured her eyes. For a moment, she stared at Dante with a reaction of neither horror nor revulsion, but one he interpreted as surprise.

Miss Hale introduced them, but the blonde did not acknowledge Dante. "I must see Dr. Warwick. My galleys and notes have disappeared."

"He is gone for the day, Dr. Arnoul. I don't know where or how he can be reached."

Outside Warwick's office, Dr. Arnoul took Dante's arm. "Mr. Dante...."

"It's Marco."

"And I am Sandrine. Please come with me. Perhaps you will be able to deduce what happened to my manuscript. I do not know what to think. I would like to hear your thoughts on the matter."

Dante hesitated. He didn't know what the hell she was talking about. He had appointments to keep in the City, his shrink at 10 AM and he wanted to be at *The Anxious Asp* by one in the afternoon. Dante noted Sandrine did not use contractions, and she had a slight accent, French, he guessed given her surname.

Sandrine removed her glasses. "Please, Marco."

Madon', those unusual viridian green eyes, her flawless features. Dante thought Sandrine to be the most stunning woman he'd ever seen. Yet despite her surface smile and lack of reaction to his marred face, he sensed a coldness that sent a shiver along his spine. She appeared more marble statue than human, a masterpiece of face and form without any warmth. He had to portray her on canvas.

Dante listened to Sandrine's story until he checked his watch. "I've stayed longer than I intended."

"I am certain we shall meet again, and soon."

The tone of Sandrine's last words sounded ominous to Dante and not flirtatious.

***

10 AM Michele's English teacher called her students row by row to take a copy of *Silas Marner* from the floor for their next book report and told the class to begin reading.

Michele began reading the first chapter of the novel until she went into a trance. She visualized *La Blond d'Hiver,* this time not in a painting. Michele had not known she was so tall. The blonde-haired person was speaking to a man of more height than she, and Michele had a glimpse of a face that suggested a skull.

Next, Michele thought she was in the library at home with the same brass bowl on a tripod on one side of the desk. A chimera sculpture like Goji and another of an Egyptian cat goddess stood atop it.

A man Michele had not seen before sat in the same chair she and Aunt Madeleine used, eyes closed. He had a gray beard. His clothes were of an older century. The elder awakened and smiled as if he could see Michele.

The school bell rang ending the period and Michele's

visions. It was time for the fifteen-minute mid-morning Nutrition Break.

Michele left the classroom and found a quiet corner in the school library to think about the significance of her first daytime trance. It had come without warning, presaging an imminent meeting with *La Blond d'Hiver* and *Le Crâne*.

Most important of all, Michele knew the identity of the elderly man.

***

Two days earlier, Dante made a 10 AM appointment with the last psychiatrist to evaluate him at Letterman Army Hospital, Dr. Laurence Monash, a short, thin, graying man in his late fifties, now back in private practice.

Monash's well-furnished suite included comfortable leather chairs, a chaise lounge, and a cluttered mahogany desk. A large blue Tabriz rug, designed with abstract animals and rosettes, laid on a shiny wood floor from desk to door. Heavy drapes bracketed a window that provided a fourth-floor view of Union Square on the corner of Geary and Powell.

Before sitting, Dante placed a painting and charcoal drawing against a bookcase, versos facing out.

"I did not expect to see you again, Mr. Dante. Two patients canceled their appointments, so I can give you two hours of my time."

Monash prepared to write on a legal pad, his recording device on.

Dante spoke in a monotone. "I rose at six as usual. I was in the bathroom, and an instant later, so it seemed, I stood in the reception office of the Comparative Literature Department at U.C. Berkeley, in front of the secretary. I could not remember leaving home and driving across the Bay to Cal. I believed I was dreaming, and then reality kicked in. What compelled me to visit the campus?"

Monash stopped writing, "Subconscious nostalgia for the campus life you led?"

"I don't think so."

"Go on."

"I wanted to leave. Something I can't explain kept me rooted in front of the departmental secretary, Miss Hale. Then a stunning tall angry blonde burst in. Her name is Dr. Sandrine Arnoul. She demanded to see Dean Nelson Warwick. Miss Hale said he would be off campus for the day and did not know where he could be reached. I could move again, and outside in the hall, Sandrine told me why she was upset. Last night she finished proofing a galley for a book she'd written, celebrated with champagne, and fell asleep at her desk. This morning, everything was gone: the galley, all her notes, and papers for another book. I wished her luck finding the galley and left."

"Continue, please."

"I can't stop thinking about her. Sandrine did not use contractions and had a slight French accent. She is a winter blonde, about six feet in flats. Unusual viridian green eyes. Flawless features. I thought her to be a masterpiece of face and form but without warmth."

"And you intend to paint her."

"Yes, but she is not the reason I asked for an appointment. You know I began to paint as therapy in the hospitals. Turned out I do have some talent. My canvases have been on sale at *The Anxious Asp*." Dante saw Monash's look of confusion and explained it was a nightspot in North Beach.

"*The Anxious Asp* ... a most interesting name."

"Aldo Serafino, the owner, was a client and close friend of my father. Serafino liked my paintings and suggested I hang them on the walls of his club. They sold out, and I'm delivering more today. He's investing in a gallery next door to promote my acrylics and graphics."

Monash gestured at the bookcase. "Have you brought some of your *oeuvres* for me to see?"

Dante left his seat and showed Monash a vivid acrylic impasto of a cable car rising from a steep hill with the Bay and Alcatraz in the background.

"Suggests Van Gogh, but still original. Bright, cheerful evidence of a healthy mind."

"It's typical of my painting, or it was." Dante handed Monash a charcoal portrait. "Beginning last Friday morning, I have drawn this woman dozens of times without wanting to."

Monash studied the lady. "So realistic, such haunted eyes."

"The sketches were not delineated at first. The last few have been more detailed, like this one."

"Who is she?"

"I've never seen her before. I feel as if I am in a vortex that is pulling me into a deep abyss. Am I crazy?"

Monash held Dante's charcoal drawing. "No, not crazy. May I keep this and study it? I assure you, Mr. Dante, you are not going mad. I believe this woman wants to find you. She may have some exceptional psychic powers. Yes, that can be the logical explanation. You may meet her in the very near future."

How could Monash be so certain? "Then, can you explain what happened to me this morning? What impelled me to drive to Cal?"

"Be logical. What was the most significant incident after

you arrived?"

Dante patted his moist brow with a handkerchief. "I had no reason to see Dean Warwick or the secretary. Sandrine's last words and tone did sound ominous 'Marco, I am certain we shall meet again, and soon.' Do you think she was seeking me, like the lady I've been drawing?"

Monash turned off the recorder and put his pad in a drawer. "Perhaps. I must review today's session first." Monash wrote on the back of a business card and gave it to Dante. "My home phone number and address." Monash glanced at the charcoal drawing. "Contact me day or night."

CHAPTER 9
SECRETS OF THE GREAT PYRAMID

It was as if time passed faster than an eye blink. Sandrine sat troubled in her '41 red Chevrolet coupe parked on Union between Fillmore and Webster outside a bakery. Now conscious of her surroundings, she could not remember anything that happened after her encounter with Marco Dante, not even driving across the Bay Bridge into the City, and now it was 1 in the afternoon. What had happened? How had she gotten here?

Sandrine left her car, entered the bakery, and purchased a loaf of warm sourdough bread. At the counter she read business cards and advertisements for adjacent businesses. A throwaway notice about a lecture on Pyramidology in a hall above the bakery interested Sandrine.

Moments later, unaware she climbed the steps, Sandrine stood at the top. A lavender-and-lace blue-haired lady sat at a pamphlet-laden table. A nearby poster on a tripod advertised:

THE SOCIETY OF THE TEN
PRESENT AT 1 PM
Dr. Astrid Lambert, noted Pyramidologist
who will discuss prophecies of the
GREAT PYRAMID
and
BRITISH-ISRAEL REVELATION
Members $1.00   Non-Members $2.50

Sandrine peered into the lecture hall. To her astonishment, she saw Warwick seated in the first row. She could not get to him. The aisle was filled with people blocking access to the front. Why was this professor, a rational thinker, attending a lecture on Pyramid Prophecy?

Sandrine paid and took one the few available seats in the last row. All around her, she heard conversations on Astrology, Pyramid and Bible prophecy, various seers, and sundry other aspects of the occult.

A tremor shook the building. The audience murmured when the lights went out then on again as Dr. Astrid Lambert materialized on the dais between parted opaque black drapes.

Lambert's face and physicality interested Sandrine. The woman's frizzled mouse-brown hair coiled above a fleshless face. Her narrow cat's eyes reflected amber under fluorescent lights. The nostrils of her thin nose flared with each breath. Upper front teeth protruded. Scrawny to the point of emaciation, she had an unhealthy, transparent, yellowish complexion. A chain and patterned medallion of gold hung to her mid-section, breaking the monotony of her floor-length robe of midnight blue.

Lambert stood beside a blackboard with a colored and detailed drawing of the Great Pyramid that included printed dates and figures. She tapped a pointer against the board. "Good afternoon and welcome to my second lecture in this series on the Great Pyramid."

Sandrine listened with much skepticism to Lambert who described advanced civilizations unfamiliar to but a few that existed 10,000 to 40,000 years before any known history of Egypt. Lambert asserted that one of them constructed the Great Pyramid. She added information Sandrine had read before.

"Belief in the Great Pyramid as a highly developed scientific instrument and as a prophecy goes back many centuries. It influenced Sir Isaac Newton and other rational philosophers of the Age of Reason. That included the founding fathers of the United States, which explains why that same pyramid is on our paper currency. Secular scientists do not like to speak of it, but according to his biographers, Isaac Newton wrote more than one million words about the riddle of the Godhead, his failed lifetime search for a hidden code in the Bible revealing the future of mankind. Newton believed the Great Pyramid's dimensions mirrored the cosmos, and he used the Book of Daniel to calculate the Apocalypse would occur after the year 3020."

Lambert paused to drink from a glass of water when the blue-hair handed out printed copies of the Great Pyramid as drawn on the blackboard.

"Today, I will refute the theory that the Great Pyramid was constructed as a tomb. Unfortunately, I must use common language so all may understand me. I ask you to study these ventilation shafts provided for the so-called Chamber of the King and Chamber of the Queen. Look. Two ventilation shafts for each chamber. I ask this: Why would ventilation be necessary in chambers of the dead? And look here. A granite plug was inserted to prevent entrance by the living."

Sandrine detected a slight French accent when Dr. Lambert spoke, but heard no surprises regarding Great Pyramid theories until the woman described its interior design, which included three chambers and connecting passageways with several anomalies. The passageway leading to the King's Chamber rose to a height of thirty-six feet, but the others lacked enough height for a typical human to stand upright. Dr. Lambert went on to describe the unique interiors of the King's and Queen's Chambers.

"It is not known why they were constructed in this manner, yet most Egyptologists theorize they were tombs, even if its interior did not resemble later burial chambers with colorful paintings and hieroglyphs. If the Great Pyramid was not a tomb, then what was it?"

Dr. Lambert paused again to give her audience time to assimilate what she had told them. Sandrine conceded the woman presented her unusual material with effective theatricality. Although skeptical, she intended to research and to refresh her memory about the Great Pyramid after the lecture.

When Dr. Lambert tapped the board again and resumed the lecture, Sandrine saw her nod at Warwick. Why? Trying to imagine what relationship they might have, she half-listened to Dr. Lambert until the woman stopped speculating about the pyramid's ventilation shafts and raised her voice to emphasize her theory, which she expressed as fact.

"Yes, you are wondering what possible use could there be for ventilation shafts in a tomb. That leaves us with the one possible conclusion. These ventilation shafts were created for a future age to use. The builders planned for the Great Pyramid's secrets to be studied and understood by enlightened members of a later civilization. The Great Pyramid is not a tomb. The Great Pyramid is a prophecy."

Lambert drank from a glass of water and savored her audience's excitement. She wrote on the board and resumed her lecture. "Here are the external measurements of the Great Pyramid. It has a total base circumference of 36,524 inches. If we erase the comma and add a decimal *here*, we have 365.24, the precise measurement of the solar year." She underlined 365.24 and wrote the original number 36,524 beside it. "Returning to the base circumference, when we divide it by 4, we have the base of each side at 9,131 inches for the time between each equinox. Divide 9,131 by 25, the number of inches in the Egyptian and Hebrew cubit, and we again have 365.24, our solar year. Also included in the dimensions of the Great Pyramid are the value of Pi, the polar diameter of the earth, and other mathematical and astronomical data I shall be covering in subsequent lectures. Oh yes, and one other important fact The Great Pyramid stands at the exact latitudinal center of the earth. I repeat ... the entire structure is a prophecy."

Lambert coughed to clear her throat. "With the base circumference figure of 36,524 in mind, we take an inch to represent one year. Using mathematical and cosmological data handed down through the centuries, and armed with our knowledge of a displacement factor of 286.1 inches, which was a builder's error and prevented the headstone from being placed, the passage system can be interpreted prophetically."

She hesitated when the lights dimmed again. Sandrine thought it odd Warwick sat motionless because everyone else around him tensed and looked toward the exit.

Lambert rapped on her board. "Please, calm yourselves. Now then, this Entrance Passage covers the time from its construction in 2625 BC to the Hebrews' Exodus from Egypt in 1486 BC. The First Ascending Passage extends from the point marking the Exodus to the date of the Crucifixion. And finally, moving up to the King's Chamber, we encounter the remaining prophecies dealing with our planet to the critical years of the Final Battle, any time between now and 2020. However, to digress a moment. The Great Pyramid has solved the mystery of the supposedly lost Ten Tribes of Israel."

A stronger tremor silenced Lambert, and the hall went dark. When the lights came on again, Sandrine left her chair. Warwick had disappeared. The parted drapes behind Lambert exposed a second exit. Before Lambert resumed her lecture, Sandrine ran to the exit and down the rear stairs, which took her outside into a deserted alley. She shouted Warwick's name and ran around the building to the street.

Sandrine went into each of the open businesses on the block. No one admitted to having seen a gray-haired man in a silver and black checked jacket. *The House of Books* was closed. For the first time, Sandrine noticed the books and pamphlets in its window display consisted of occult subject matter.

Lambert's audience exited the building, and Sandrine stopped one of the men. "What happened?"

"Dr. Lambert canceled the lecture because the tremors upset her, but they refunded our money."

"Is Dr. Lambert still there?"

"No, she left too."

Sandrine found a pay phone and called Warwick's office. Miss Hale had not returned from lunch. She doubted the secretary would appear at her desk the way things were going.

First, her book galley and notes, and now Warwick had vanished. Was it all somehow connected? Sandrine believed so. How best to proceed? The answer came in an instant.

CHAPTER 10
GALERIA SERAFINO

On Monday, at 1 PM, Dante parked at the yellow curb loading zone in front of *The Anxious Asp* on Columbus near Broadway. He carried his canvases and an artist's sketchpad into the adjacent *Galeria Serafino* and placed them on the industrial strength forest-green carpet along a rosewood-paneled wall that held several of his paintings.

Aldo Serafino, a streetwise hard-guy from New York's Hell's Kitchen, came from the back room and assessed Dante's work. "Yeah, good, Marco, but, is this all? Six measly oils? Don't get me wrong, they're great; but understand this, you've got less than five months before the exhibit, and in a couple of weeks I have to begin printing catalogs, price lists, and mailers."

"There's four more drying at home."

"Not enough."

Dante handed Serafino the sketchpad and described how he could draw nothing else for the past several days.

Serafino studied each page. "Weird. Creepy." He

47

returned the pad to Dante. "Come with me. You've got plenty of work to do."

They went to the rear of the gallery into a framing and shipping room. A six-foot seven-inch bearded redhead in fringed leather gave Dante a greeting hug short of crushing his ribs.

Dante had played end for Lowell and Cal at the same time Rafe Mazurek played tackle for St. Ignatius High School and USC as the Trojans' top hatchet man. Mazurek was their designated player to take out the opposing team's offensive star. He did the same in the pros for the Chicago Bears until a knee injury sidelined the redhead for good and kept him out of the draft.

Mazurek next found work in film and TV appearing in non-speaking tough-guy roles until he was arrested as the prime suspect in a studio murder even though his priors had been druken disorderlies, mostly classic barroom brawls. Dante's father proved the murderer framed Mazurek and helped the cops catch the real perp. He brought the six foot seven inch giant to Serafino who hired him as a bouncer. When Dante first displayed his paintings at *The Anxious Asp*, they discovered Mazurek was a natural framer.

"Over here, Marco." Serafino showed Dante a mock-up promotional poster for the exhibit, a color photo in which he stood beside an oil of a sailboat tacking on choppy San Francisco Bay with Alcatraz in the background.

"Looks great, Al."

Serafino gave Dante a pencil and pointed at stacks of serigraphs on several long rectangular tables. Mazurek left to find more wood for the frames.

Dante signed and numbered the serigraphs, a dull but necessary chore for any artist, until Serafino's phone at the same instant.

"Marco, do me a favor. See who it is."

***

Dr. Monash was right.

In the gallery showroom, Dante gaped at the woman he could not stop drawing. She was staring at his paintings. The same hair, large and sad eyes, every feature of his sketches had been accurate. The woman faced Dante and exhaled as if relieved of a great burden.

"*Le Crâne.*"

Dante did not understand what she said.

She pointed at the signature on one of his oils. "You are Marco Antonio Dante."

"That's right."

"Yes, everything is much clearer now. You have great sensitivity, powerful emotions. You are receptive to thoughts from others."

So Monash had said.

"My calculations have been confirmed. You are a Cancer, and your ascendant sign is ... I see you are skeptical. You ought not to be hostile toward Judicial Astrology. The stars can tell us much."

"Why don't you start by telling me who you are?"

"I am Mrs. Madeleine Desaix."

"Your initials, D.A., what names do they represent?"

"You do not speak French?"

"No."

"That is most unfortunate. It will complicate matters. Although my name is pronounced D.A., it is spelled D-e-s-a-i-x. It has been a long and exhausting search. You, Marco Antonio Dante, you are *Le Crâne.*"

"I'm who?"

"That will be revealed to you later."

Dante opened his sketchpad and showed Mrs. Desaix her portraits. "Why have I been drawing you?"

"Be assured, Mr. Dante, now that we have met, you shall no longer be compelled to draw me." Mrs. Desaix's eyes became unfocused. "I now see you with a young woman of great beauty. White-blonde hair of winter frost."

The way things had been going, Dante was not surprised that Mrs. Desaix described Sandrine.

"Here is my address. It is essential you come to my home tonight, Mr. Dante."

He stuffed the paper into his jacket pocket without reading it. "What is it you really want?"

"I cannot explain until we meet again."

Because Dante had lacked control over his hands, he could not dismiss Mrs. Desaix as a harmless eccentric. "Can't you be more specific?"

Mrs. Desaix opened the gallery door and pointed at Dante. "*O quels horribles calamités, changements.* If you do not come, we are lost, lost, all of us lost, forever lost."

The gallery shook, and Dante reached for the wall. A bright red flash of light blinded him. By the time he regained his sight, Mrs. Desaix had disappeared.

Dante stepped outside. Street traffic moved at a normal pace along Columbus. Employees and shoppers from adjacent businesses were on the sidewalk talking about the quake.

Serafino stood in the gallery doorway. "Bet it was no more than a five-point-three. Nothing to worry about, Marco. No damage."

At least the shaker had been real. Dante wasn't sure about Mrs. Desaix.

***

4 PM, Monday afternoon, Michele finished her book report on *Silas Marner* and faced the malachite chimera on her desk. Goji had become Michele's best friend, the one creature in whom she confided. "Goji, there are too many coming events I cannot see. Who ... what is the shadow Aunt Madeleine mentioned this morning?"

Golden light emanated from the gargoyle's eyes. In the brass bowl on the tripod at the side of the desk, water continued to ripple and branches moved even though the tremors ceased.

Michele experienced weightlessness, as if out of body. As in her dreams and nightmares, she witnessed confusing occurrences. Some Michele recognized from her history lessons. Warfare. Assassinations. Fire, flood, famine, earthquakes, and pestilence. Other images appeared to be both past and futuristic with strange humanoids, vehicles, machines, weapons, and clothing.

Which was the past? Which was the future? Time and space had no meaning until she saw Aunt Madeleine dead and the time on the 400-day clock in the library. Unless she could change the future, her aunt would die at 10:27 PM tonight.

Michele thought about the two individuals Aunt Madeleine mentioned and whom she had seen earlier, the beautiful *La Blond d'Hiver* and *Le Crâne*. Michele closed her eyes and tried to take another journey through time and space, but no further revelations came, nor any automatic writing. Neither had puberty, which Aunt Madeleine often said would bring to her The Understanding.

THE SORCERESS AND THE SKULL

Michele gazed again into Goji's eyes. "Why can I not see the future whenever I wish? Why must I wait for it to come to me?"

***

Mrs. Desaix entered the library, surprised to see Michele at the desk. "Still studying? It is past five. Are you having trouble with your school work?"

She rose and kissed her aunt. "No, I wanted to finish my book report. Before that, I prepared our *Goûter*. It is in the kitchen."

"We shall have it later." Mrs. Desaix placed her purse on the desk, sat, and removed several documents from a legal size envelope. She spoke in French. "I want to show you something of great importance. Come, stand beside me, and read my notarized Last Will and Testament with instructions for your future. You are the sole inheritor of our family estate. I have placed copies in a safety deposit box at our bank. It contains many valuables, available money, and the codes for your Swiss accounts. You already have signatures and access to them, but because you are not of legal age, you must have a guardian and executor to guide and protect you after I die."

"*Le Crâne?*"

"Yes. Today I found him. His name is Marco Antonio Dante. He lives nearby. I had long ago prepared these documents in English and French before I learned who he was. After I had met Monsieur Dante, I added his name to these documents at the bank, my signature, the date, and had them notarized."

Mrs. Desaix placed the papers in a desk drawer, locked it, and gave Michele one of the keys. "They will be here when

52

you need them. Tonight, you shall meet *Le Crâne*, and perhaps..." Mrs. Desaix closed her eyes, "... yes, definitely, *La Blond d'Hiver*."

CHAPTER 11
REVELATIONS

That evening, a completed portrait, unlike Dante's impastos of San Francisco and the Bay, dried on an easel. Its subject, a pallid young beauty with viridian eyes, wore a white headdress of Renaissance style and surreal design that blended into a frosty Italianate archway, with a background of diminishing ivory icy arches. He signed and dated it on the bottom front, and again on the verso with a title, *The Winter Blonde*. Mié hissed at the canvas and ran from the studio. Odd, the Abyssinian never critiqued his paintings before.

After Dante changed into street clothes, he settled in the den with a scotch and ice. Ensconced in her favorite armchair opposite him, Mié meowed a question.

The doorbell rang, accompanied by persistent knocking. Yes the way his day had been going, he was not surprised to see Sandrine, pale as his portrait, standing in the swirling mist outside in a hooded black wool overcoat. Why was he not attracted to the stunning blonde? Mié had a more violent reaction. The Abyssinian bounded from her armchair, hissed at Sandrine, and leaped onto the mantle above the dormant fireplace. There she tensed as if to spring.

Sandrine ignored Mié, rejected Dante's offer of a drink, and related an experience identical to what had happened to him earlier in the day. She remembered nothing after their brief conversation outside Warwick's office suite until she had crossed the Bay Bridge and parked on Union between Fillmore and Webster in an unfamiliar neighborhood. Sandrine next told Dante about Warwick's attendance and disappearance at a lecture on Pyramid Prophecy.

"Marco, he never returned to his office, nor has he answered his home phone since."

Warwick was not Dante's concern. "How did you find me, and why?"

"I found your address amongst old files in the Administration Building. Why, you asked? I cannot say."

Dante chose not to tell Sandrine about his blackout earlier in the morning. Instead, he showed her the sketchpad and described how he could draw Mrs. Desaix and nothing else until she appeared at *Galeria Serafino*.

"She said I had a female companion with hair of winter frost and pleaded with me to be at her home before midnight."

Sandrine's inscrutable countenance never changed from the moment she arrived, nor did it now when she said, "Then I must go with you, Marco."

***

Dante and Sandrine approached a Victorian house looming through a thick San Francisco mist. No cars traversed the wet street. No one was visible on the sidewalk. No sounds came from behind the drawn drapes of neighboring houses, but mournful foghorns broke the silence.

Before Dante and Sandrine reached the top step, the front door opened. A slight, pale, pre-pubescent girl about five feet tall stood framed in the doorway, dressed as a typical teen in a white blouse, burgundy cashmere cardigan and pleated plaid skirt. Under straight, night-black hair cut gamine-short, large brown eyes dominated her face. She introduced herself as Michele, Mrs. Desaix's niece, said they were expected, and ushered them inside.

Michele closed, locked, and bolted the front door behind them. Dante and Sandrine followed the girl through a living room filled with antique furniture and valuable Old Master paintings on the wall to a spacious library. Michele closed the double pocket doors.

Dante scanned the library. The far wall contained an ornate marble fireplace, from which flames warmed the room. A seventeenth-century Dutch painting of a pastoral scene hung above a 400-day clock on the mantel.

Bound leather tomes filled shelves from the beamed ceiling to a parquet floor covered with Oriental rugs. Two black and orange flower-patterned mohair armchairs faced an ebony desk and upholstered high-back chair in front of drawn drapes. A dictionary-size book lay open on a desktop lectern.

Sandrine went to a tripod supporting a brass bowl beside the desk half-filled with water and branches. She could not take her eyes from it, as if searching for something specific rather than glancing in casual curiosity.

One Persian hand-knotted masterpiece similar to the rug in Dr. Monash's office held Dante's attention. Giving the effect of a kaleidoscopic optical illusion, the main pattern of rosettes, tendrils, and cloudbursts in the center appeared to merge and form a five-pointed star, and he recognized Hebrew letters in each of the triangles.

On the verge of a dizzy spell, Dante saw a malachite chimera he had not noticed before atop the desk. Without a doubt, it was the same bloody creature that appeared in his studio window the other night.

Dante touched the chimera, and a bright light emanated from its eyes. Was it an acknowledgment of recognition? He pulled his hand away when its body throbbed.

Mrs. Desaix parted the doors and entered, wearing a burgundy velvet caftan. Michele followed and sat on a mohair sofa near the fire. She thanked Dante for coming, addressed Sandrine as *La Blond d'Hiver,* then suggested they dispense with formalities and use first names.

When Madeleine sat in the high back chair, Sandrine settled in the armchair closest to the tripod and brass bowl. Dante preferred to stand for the time being. He had not seen Michele place the chimera on the mantel next to the 400-day clock. Or perhaps it had moved by itself. Anything seemed possible. Had he awakened this morning in a parallel world of inexplicable occurrences and coincidences?

Madeleine did not look as old and harried to Dante as she had in his sketches and their meeting earlier in the day at *Galeria Serafino.* She was well groomed and attractive, and he guessed her to be middle to late thirties.

Dante's neck felt as if it was burning. He saw Michele staring at him with those large inscrutable brown eyes. Something indefinable about the girl caused Dante to feel protective.

Madeleine lit a *Galois* and opened the top center drawer. She handed Dante a sheet of vellum on which a quatrain had been penned:

THE SORCERESS AND THE SKULL

De sang Bisance, garde seront yeux penetrants,
Descouvrirant de loin la Blond d'Hiver;
Elle et le Crâne, au parc enclin seront entrans,
Feu, sang verser, eau de sang colorer.

She translated for Dante from memory:

Of Byzantine blood, penetrating eyes shall be on guard,
Discovering from afar the Winter Blonde;
She and the Skull shall enter the sloping park,
Fire, bloodshed, water colored by blood."

Dante noticed that Madeleine had translated *la Blond d'Hiver* as the Winter Blonde, the same title he wrote on Sandrine's portrait.

Madeleine said, "Given your disfigured face, and forgive me if I offend, you are *Le Crâne*, the Skull, mentioned in the quatrain."

On impulse, Dante touched the taut skin of his restructured face. He looked again at the words on the vellum. "Madeleine, this resembles quatrains written by Nostradamus I read years ago in books about him."

Madeleine chain-lit another cigarette. "You are correct, Marco. My niece and I of necessity have used many aliases. My true name is Madeleine Celeste de Nostredame. We are direct descendants of Nostradamus."

Sandrine's silence and icy demeanor puzzled Dante. She had yet to say a word.

"Who is The Byzantine mentioned in this quatrain?"

"An unknown adversary, Marco, named as such in Nostradamus' unpublished prophecies. The Byzantine is near. That villain will murder to acquire the prophecies and other secrets, meant for Michelle alone. Other quatrains in my possession foretell that you, *le Crâne*, are destined to protect Michele from The Byzantine. That is why I asked you to be here before midnight. I have devoted my life to safeguarding my niece. Her survival is now in your hands."

Water churned in the brass bowl. Michele spoke in a monotone as her eyes became unfocused. *"C'est vrai, c'est vrai. Destitué ... la Dame farouche... mort et cris ... horreurs extrêmes ... tradiment ... sang effusion ... sera muertri ...."* The girl went silent and sat, alert and tense on the edge of the couch.

The chimera no longer occupied the mantel. It had returned to its original place on the desk.

Dante did not waste time asking Sandrine what Michele said. "Madeleine, where are the quatrains that identify The Byzantine, and how I am supposed to protect your niece?" "Clues do exist amongst the unpublished prophecies written for me, for Michele, and in other prophecies concerning the two of you."

"The two of us? You're saying Nostradamus wrote prophecies about Sandrine and me four hundred years ago?"

"Yes, he did, as in that quatrain you hold in your hands. Please do not be impatient, Marco. My time is short, and I have much of the greatest importance to show you."

Madeleine reached into the middle drawer and placed two legal documents on the desk. From a side drawer, she took out a large envelope and several loose vellum sheets, which she placed next to her will and an authorization.

"I ...."

CHAPTER 12
EMERGENT

At 10:27 PM Monday night, Madeleine collapsed in her chair. The 400-day clock stopped. Foghorns sounded a lugubrious lament.

"Elle est morte." Michele stood at her aunt's side.

Sandrine followed. Marco checked Madeleine's pulse, closed her eyes, and used the phone on the desk. Michele heard him speaking to someone named Doyle before he hung up the phone and returned to her aunt.

"Inspector Conlon will be here soon, Michele. Have you a relative or friend of the family we can notify?"

"No one, Marco."

"Is there anything we can do for you?"

"No, I have been prepared for this moment." Michele held the top loose sheet of vellum and showed it to Marco. "This quatrain foretold Aunt Madeleine's passing and time of death."

Madeleine, Madeleine, gardes toi

DONALD MICHAEL PLATT

le plus proche ombre noir,
Pres le Cite de Saint Francis sera conflit donne;
Sang espandu, le plus grand fille a main,
L'enfant ne sexe sera pardonne.

Michele translated for Marco:
"Madeleine, Madeleine, guard yourself from the dark
shadow,
Near the City of Saint Francis shall be the conflict;
Blood shall be spilled, the greatest daughter taken,
Neither child nor sex shall be spared."

Michele saw Sandrine attempt to read the next quatrain
lying on the desk. She gathered the loose papers and
envelope, put them in a drawer, and locked it. Michele next
suggested they go to the adjacent living room and wait there
for Marco's police inspector friend to arrive. She closed the
pocket doors behind leaving Goji on the desk.

In the dim and cold great room, Michele lit a fire and
went to the kitchen. She returned several minutes later with
an ornate silver service containing teabags, carafes of hot
water and coffee, and petit fours. She set the tray on an
antique coffee table in front of an upholstered Queen Anne
sofa where Sandrine sat facing the fire between two
matching love seats. Michele thought the Winter Blonde
looked beautiful all in black, her perfect features frozen as a
statue. *Mais oui, elle était la dame maléfice.*

Marco stood by the alabaster mantel smoking a pipe. The
play of firelight against his skull-like face gave him a
menacing mien, but he was no threat. On the contrary,
Michele knew they shared an unbreakable bond, which he
would soon discover and come to accept.

She poured a cup of tea, selected a petit four, and stood

61

by the side of the mantel opposite Marco. Although alone at age thirteen, Michele faced her future calm, confident, and in control. A new phase in her life had begun.

After tea, Michele went into the library and returned with two documents she gave to Dante. The first was Madeleine's notarized Last Will and Testament, written both in English and in French. She had appointed Dante to be Michele's guardian and trustee until age twenty-one. In the second document, she named him executor.

***

Now Michele's guardian, executor, and protector, Dante became concerned his new responsibilities might affect his time at the easel.

Conlon arrived. Dante made the introductions, and Michele led the inspector into the library where he went to Madeleine. Michele stood close to Dante at the desk.

Sandrine asked Conlon if she could leave. He asked a few cursory questions, wrote on his pad her address, home and work phone numbers, and gave Sandrine permission to go.

"Time of death, Marco?"

Dante pointed at the mantel and told Conlon the 400-day clock stopped the instant Madeleine died.

"Pretty lady. So young." Conlon reached for the phone. "Calling the necropolis." After hanging up, he took Dante aside out of Michele's hearing. "What were you and Sandrine doing here? And by the way, Marco, you look exhausted."

"I feel worse. You left me about three in the morning. I fell asleep around four and awakened at six to the strangest day of my life."

Dante summarized his being compelled to create charcoal sketches of Madeleine Desaix; the morning blackout until he became aware of his surroundings at Dwinelle Hall where he'd met Sandrine; his two-hour appointment with Dr. Monash, Madeleine's arrival at the gallery, and her plea for him to come to her home before midnight.

"Where does Sandrine fit into all this?"

"Doyle, I haven't finished. First, I could again paint without any psychic interference from Madeleine Desaix. Around seven Sandrine came to my home ostensibly to discuss the disappearance of Dean Nelson Warwick. I believe she had an ulterior motive. Sandrine accompanied me after I told her Madeleine insisted I come here before midnight. She believed I was someone called the Skull and Sandrine the Winter Blonde. Both of us are mentioned in quatrains written for Michele by their ancestor, the prophet Nostradamus."

"Nostradamus? Are you kidding me, Marco?"

"I wish, and then there's this, Doyle." Dante gave Conlon the two legal documents naming him Michele's guardian, trustee, and estate executor. "And I am supposed to protect her against a foe known as The Byzantine, all that foretold in the prophecies."

Conlon stopped writing. "Marco, we'll need a fuller interview sometime tomorrow after you've had a good night's sleep."

"What do we do with Michele?"

"The documents look legit. She is your ward now. We don't want her in the system and placed in foster care." Conlon glanced at Michele sipping tea on the couch. "The girl is unnaturally calm."

"It is her way. She is a peculiar child."

"She can't stay here alone. You'll have to take Michaele home with you."

Dante wished he could think of a viable alternative.

"We can sort out the legal stuff later, Marco. You have no idea who The Byzantine might be?"

"No."

"The girl?

"Michele doesn't know either, but she believes his identity can be found in her personal quatrains."

***

The Woman drank aged Port and smoked a cigar at her desk. Earlier in the evening, a subordinate called to say he located the house where Michele lived. At eleven-thirty, an ambulance and squad car arrived. Pretending to be a reporter, he learned from a policeman that the lady of the house had died, most likely Michele's Aunt Madeleine. When the Woman asked about Michele, he said the girl disappeared earlier, and he did not know where she had been taken, or by whom.

CHAPTER 13
A NEW NORMAL

It was past midnight. Mié rubbed against Michele's legs, purred at maximum revs, and scratched the suitcase Dante had carried into one of the spare bedrooms on the second floor. He lifted the cat and set her on the dresser.

"Mié, behave yourself."

"So fitting, Marco, that you named her for one of the Egyptian cat goddesses." Michele opened her suitcase and removed the chimera. "Mié, meet your new friend Goji."

Mié sniffed and rubbed her cheeks against the figure's malachite surface.

Dante left Michele. Downstairs in the den, he lit the fireplace, filled his pipe with fresh tobacco, and poured cognac into a snifter. After settling in an armchair, Dante imagined what life would be like with the enigmatic girl who would be living with him until age twenty-one. No, not really a girl, except chronologically.

From the moment of Madeleine's passing, Michele's demeanor became serene and mature.

THE SORCERESS AND THE SKULL

She came into the den with Mié at her heels. The cat leaped onto the fireplace mantel. Michele took the sketchpad Dante left propped against the wall by the fireplace and intended to burn. He cursed himself for not destroying the sketches of her aunt.

Michele flipped through his drawings of Madeleine. Dante blinked several times. His last charcoal sketch had become a pastel.

The fire warmed the den to a cozy ambiance. Moisture collected on the windows. Outside, foghorns sounded. Dante and Michele sat silent, facing each other. She continued to turn pages of the sketchpad. He shut his eyes, lifted both legs atop an ottoman, and relaxed for the first time since awakening to a day of odd occurrences.

Mié made an unusual sound. Dante looked at the mantel and saw Goji beside her. The play of light in the room emphasized the beauty of Goji's malachite form. Swirls, circles, and wavy lines, from the lightest to darkest intense shades of green, fascinated him. Goji's open luminous golden eyes fixed on Dante. In the same firelight, Mié's coat reflected burnished copper.

Dante finished his cognac and told Michele to get some sleep because they had a full morning ahead. She obeyed and took the sketchpad to her room. At the door to his suite across the hall, Dante felt an obsessive need to paint and went to his studio. He completed a new portrait in less than fifteen minutes.

The inexplicable had become the new normal.

***

Michele awakened at her usual time: five in the morning. She kissed Goji's forehead and gave Mié a generous stroking.

After bathing and dressing for the day, she went to the kitchen where she fed and watered Mié. Marco's refrigerator was well stocked, but the pantry lacked many essentials, specifically petit fours for an afternoon *Goûter*.

She made breakfast for Marco and herself: cheese omelets, toast with orange marmalade, and strong black coffee. She planned to make him breakfast every day and cook other meals, if he so wished.

They had a full morning ahead and arrived at Lowell at eight in the morning. She was delighted to learn Marco had graduated from the same high school. They met first with Principal Stephens, who did not recognize Dante at first, but well remembered him when he was able to see past the disfigurement. Stephens praised Michele as one of the most academically advanced students he'd encountered, and suggested she transfer to a university in the fall despite her age. He recommended Stanford. Dante preferred Cal. Michele announced her intention to major in archeology and ancient writings.

The Principal accompanied them to the Attendance Office and each of Michele's classrooms to notify the registrar and her teachers the change in guardianship, address, and phone number. Michele took pleasure in both faculty and classmates' reactions to Marco. His face, height, and physicality had an air of menace that intimidated all.

Dante told each teacher he was the only adult allowed to remove Michele from class and that she would not attend school today.

***

Dante drove Michele from Lowell to Montgomery Street and his lawyers' office suite. He spoke to his father's partners about probating Madeleine's will, getting the Court to grant him immediate Powers of Attorney, and arranging for Madeleine's cremation. While the lawyers questioned Michele regarding the will, Dante phoned Conlon and asked how soon he could have a death certificate. Conlon described his conversation with the Deputy Coroner. Because they found prescriptions for a serious heart condition in Mrs. Desaix's bedroom and bathroom, the DC wrote the cause of death as a heart attack. Conlon promised to get five copies to Dante at the end of the day.

At Wells Fargo, Dante spoke with a Lowell classmate whose father was on the bank's board of directors. A secretary made copies of Madeleine's will. As soon as Dante had papers giving him power of attorney and the death certificate, he would have access to all accounts and Madeleine's safety deposit box.

Before they went to *Galeria Serafino*, Michele asked if she could do some marketing at her favorite French bakery on Union Street, close to his and Madeleine's home. Dante waited in the car.

The owner, Madame Simone, kissed Michele's cheeks. Madeleine's neighbors had told her what happened. She offered more than condolences and gave Michele at no charge an oversize array of sweet rolls.

CHAPTER 14
BRITISH-ISRAEL TRUTH

Sandrine had left Madeleine's home in an adrenaline rush because quatrains written centuries ago mentioned her. They belonged to Michele, but Marco's appointment to be the girl's guardian was most unsettling. Gaining access to those quatrains became more difficult, and now took precedence over her missing manuscript and notes. Sandrine bypassed her apartment across the Bay in Berkeley and drove to Warwick's house in nearby Piedmont. She saw no lights, rang the doorbell several times, and knocked. No response.

Tuesday morning, most of the Comparative Literature faculty gathered in the outer office at Dwinelle Hall. No one had heard from Warwick since Friday. Miss Hale was absent too, her desk drawers bare, the top cleared except for the phone.

Campus police unlocked Warwick's office. Someone emptied his desk drawers and filing cabinet. Books filled the shelves. Sandrine found a pamphlet inserted between them:

69

"The Great Pyramid as Prophecy". She remembered seeing it in the display window of the bookstore downstairs from where Warwick disappeared. Sandrine left campus and drove across the Bay to *The House of Books* on Union in the City. Featured in the center window display of occult publications was the same pamphlet on Pyramid Prophecy she found in Warwick's office.

The dimly lit store felt like a sauna. It reeked of mildew and the musty smell of old books. Sandrine walked along the shelves reading titles. One row contained books about Nostradamus. Nothing new, she read them all years earlier. Sandrine called for someone to help her. No one responded. She went to the rear of the store, brushed past dark, moldy drapes, and stepped into another room.

A pale middle-aged man lay on his back with his head hanging over the edge of a long table. Despite the steam heat, he wore a heavy brown overcoat and muffler over a matching suit of coarse wool. Not a bead of sweat was evident on his pallid face, but Sandrine's brow dampened with perspiration.

Aware of a presence, he sat on the edge of the table. His upturned nose seemed unable to prevent sagging facial flesh from falling below the chin. "Who are you? What do you want?"

"Sorry to have disturbed you, Mr...?"

"MacAndrew, Stuart MacAndrew." He sniffed and wiped his nose with his coat sleeve, then stood. "I've had this disagreeable allergy for two weeks."

"Is that why you were closed yesterday? I was at Dr. Lambert's lecture upstairs."

"Ah, yes, she's the foremost expert on secrets of The Great Pyramid." MacAndrew sniffed, *nnncchhhhed*, and swallowed his phlegm. "Sorry about that. Blowing the nose harms the membrane."

Sandrine backed away from MacAndrew disgusted. "Dr. Lambert aborted her lecture because of the tremors. I had hoped to hear more about her theories on Pyramid Prophecy and British-Israel Revelation. How can I reach her?"

MacAndrew removed his overcoat and muffler, dropped them on a chair, and went to a small table containing a filthy ceramic pot on a hot plate. "Would you like some? It's superb chamomile tea."

Sandrine winced at the tea's unpleasant odor and rejected his offer. MacAndrew poured a cup for himself and invited her to come with him to the front of the store. "I don't have Dr. Lambert's address or phone number. What did you say you wanted?"

"I had to leave Dr. Lambert's lecture before it was over, and I missed her discussion of British-Israel Revelation."

MacAndrew became less of a buffoon. His nose was no longer stuffed. Pallor disappeared; face took on color and an obnoxious smirk. "For whom do you think the Pyramid Prophecies were created?"

"Dr. Lambert said it was for a future generation."

"Oh, yes, we were speaking of Dr. Lambert. It is no secret, you know. The prophecies of the Great Pyramid were created for Israel."

"The Jews?"

Anger altered MacAndrew's protean features. "Not for those mongrelized Jews. For True Israel."

"What's the difference?"

MacAndrew's expression changed yet again, this time from harmless crank to the malignant intensity of the true believer. In a condescending tone, he lectured Sandrine that Jews were a mixture of inferior races. Idumeans, Armenoids, Mongoloids, Khazars, and Slavs. The true Israelites, the Ten

Tribes of Israel, were never lost and maintained their racial purity throughout centuries of wandering across Asia and Europe, where they left obvious clues through names.

MacAndrew told Sandrine the Persians referred to the Israelites as children of Isaac, Saccaseni in their language, from which Saxon was derived. The seafaring tribe of Dan founded Danmark, as the Danes call their country and the Danube River. Ultimately, the Israelite tribes settled in Scandinavia and the British Isles. In the Eddas of Norse mythology, the fabulous ash-tree supported the universe and struck its roots through the worlds. They called one root rising to Asgard Yggdrasil. Israel again."

"You say the lost tribes settled in England?"

"England, yes, but also Scotland, Ireland, and Wales. Queen Victoria knew that the Royal Family, *her* family, and she were descended from King David. Prince Albert shared her knowledge. That is why all their male children since have been circumcised by a rabbi-*mohel*. Regardless of their names given at coronation, every firstborn son descended from Victoria and Albert has been baptized with the name David and called that within the family."

"Astonishing, but I must confess I find all that difficult to believe."

"Then allow me to convince you of British-Israel Truth. Téa Tephi, daughter of Zedekiah, the last King of Israel, escaped the invading Assyrians with the prophet Jeremiah. Their wandering took them to Ireland, where King Heremon fell in love with the beautiful princess. They married, and their descendants became the House of Stuart. All British royals were descended from Mary Stuart, also known as Mary Queen of Scots, through her son, James I.

"There is more. Joseph made the Bull his tribal symbol. His son, Ephraim, inherited the birthright and became

72

official leader of the Bull Tribe. As is obvious linguistically, Ephraim and Heifer come from the same word root. Therefore, it is not surprising England, which is Ephraim, has been called John Bull."

"How does your British-Israel Revelation tie in with Pyramid Prophecy?"

MacAndrew told Sandrine how Shem, son of Noah, became Pharaoh of Egypt and built the Great Pyramid under Divine Guidance, which included all the scientific data and prophetic revelation necessary for mankind to prosper. Later, during the Exodus, the tribe of Issachar took the pyramid's secrets out of Egypt."

"Does your society have a function other than to give lectures and publish?"

MacAndrew gave Sandrine additional material on the subject of British-Israel Truth. "The purpose of our society is to awaken all true Israelites, to avoid racial contamination, to fulfill our destiny as foretold in the Bible, and to prepare for the Second Coming of our Messiah." He bagged the books. "But first, we must wage a successful war against the Third Antichrist."

"Does the Third Antichrist have a name?"

MacAndrew's tone was patronizing. "The Antichrists are not necessarily individuals. They can be ideas and movements that have murdered and enslaved innocent millions. The first two Antichrists have come and gone. The Third Antichrist has many heads. The final battle is imminent. Its outcome in doubt, but it has been predicted to be resolved between the years 1999 and 2020." MacAndrew gave Sandrine his pen and a file card. "I'd like your name and address for our mailing list."

"Alice Kent." That pseudonym should be Anglo-Saxon enough for MacAndrew.

"Kent? Perfect. I knew it. Forgive me for having stared at you so intently, Miss Kent, but you have the bone structure, the coloring, and the intelligence... all the characteristics of Israelite racial purity. Please turn your head. Thank you. Yes, you display the Norse qualities of Benjamin and Dan with the Getae features of Manasseh and Ephraim."

"Imagine that." Sandrine wrote a false address.

MacAndrew showed her a chart displaying coats-of-arms for the Ten Tribes of Israel. "I will be delighted to send you copies of your tribal arms. You are entitled to four quarterings for a patch to wear on your blazer."

"I must be going. Perhaps another time."

MacAndrew handed Sandrine an engraved invitation. "But you must attend our formal dinner this Saturday evening. It is our annual event. Members will be there from all over the world. The most important people. Even Queen Victoria and Edward VII belonged to our society."

Sandrine placed the invitation in her purse. "I will do my best to attend."

MacAndrew's eyes narrowed, his tone suspicious. "It is *Miss* Kent. You aren't married."

"No, why?"

"It would be unfortunate if we had to deny anyone admission because of spousal racial impurity."

Sandrine watched for a reaction to her next question. "Is Dr. William Warwick a member of your Society?"

Not even an eye blink. "No, the name is unfamiliar, although deliciously Israelite. Why do you ask?"

"Nothing important. He is a colleague of mine, and I saw him reading one of your pamphlets on Pyramid Prophecy."

"He could have found it anywhere." MacAndrew opened the door for Sandrine. "Miss Kent, I do hope you will come to our gala. One of our special guests of honor will be Dr.

74

Hideki Yoshida, the president of our Tokyo chapter, which survived despite the recent war."

"Dr. Yoshida?"

"You know him?"

"No, but the name is Japanese. Did you not say your society endorses racial purity?"

"Of course we do, but one of the Lost Ten Tribes of Israel wandered to the East and settled throughout the islands of Nippon. Do you know anything about Linguistics?"

If you only knew. "Not a thing."

"Listen, then. Samurai is a variation of Samaria, the capital of ancient Israel. Samurai are the direct descendants of Israelites who came to Japan centuries ago. Samurai are white Japanese from the tribe of Manasseh."

Sachsen to Saxon, Dan to Denmark, Yggdrasil to Israel. MacAndrew had stood Linguistic Science on its head.

CHAPTER 15
THE LITTLE SORCERESS

Tuesday noon, Dante parked against a yellow curb in front of the *Galeria Serafino*, which was closed, and removed Sandrine's painting from the back seat. Workers were demolishing the interior of an adjacent store Serafino had purchased to expand the gallery.

An employee let Dante and Michele into *The Anxious Asp*, which opened for business at 5 PM. They passed through a lobby, bar, and cabaret where Dante's impasto paintings of San Francisco hung on the walls, to Serafino's second floor expansive office.

Dante propped Sandrine's portrait, verso out, against a wall by the entrance and introduced Michele to Serafino and Mazurek, who were having lunch at his desk. "I've been appointed Michele's legal guardian."

Both men rose. Serafino welcomed Michele to his family. He ordered lunch for Dante and Michele and showed them his extensive inventory of unframed etchings, mezzotints, and serigraphs by Picasso, Miró, Dalí, and the Impressionists

76

stored in oversize cabinet drawers. The graphics were to be displayed in the added wing of the gallery. Illustrated oversize volumes about those artists' paintings and graphics filled a pair of two-shelf bookcases.

"Can't wait to move all this to the gallery office when it's ready. Okay, let's see what you brought me." Serafino studied Sandrine's portrait from all angles, lighting, and distances. "Marco, this is great. A true masterpiece."

Serafino passed the painting to Mazurek. "Any ideas for a frame, Rafe?"

"Plenty. It's better than anything you've done, Marco."

"Good. We'll start making serigraphs." Serafino looked at the verso. "*The Winter Blonde*, a perfect title. Who's the model?"

"Someone I met at Cal yesterday."

"You got more of her, Marco?"

"In my head."

A waiter knocked on the door and brought Michele roast beef and Swiss cheese on rye with a glass of water, Dante a Reuben and a bottle of Schlitz beer.

"Michele has incredible eyes. You should paint her portrait in your new style."

"I already have, Al. Back in a moment."

Last night during his less than fifteen-minute flurry of creativity, Dante painted Michele full face to emphasize those eyes, with Mié below her chin, against a medieval tapestry background of mythical beasts and alchemists' paraphernalia. He opened the trunk of his car where the portrait lay face up and stepped back. "What the...?"

Goji had been added to the portrait, feline face above Michele's head, eyes open. Wet when he placed the painting in the trunk this morning, dry now, Dante did not remember including the chimera.

77

He carried Michele's portrait into the office. "This is The Little Sorceress."

Serafino took the painting. "Love it. That creature ...."

"It's a gargoyle, Al."

"So many rich greens. And the cat! Different colors, of course, but their eyes are identical to Michele's. A stroke of genius. I want more in your new style."

Michele looked at the painting with a smile more enigmatic than the Mona Lisa, and Dante remembered she had not seen it until now.

"Marco, I am pleased you included Goji."

"How could I not? By the way, Al, can I borrow a truck and two of your schleppers for the afternoon? I have to move a huge desk, all Michele's clothes, and things she wants to my house. It's a block up the hill and around the corner from me."

Mazurek volunteered and promised to bring a pair of bouncers from *The Anxious Asp* to help.

The men discussed the best place to hang the two portraits in the gallery, and Michele selected a book about the Fauvists from one of the shelves. She leafed through it and lingered at a landscape by Derain. Michele had not seen the painting before, yet a powerful force pulled her into the scene.

The Provençal countryside was bright and cheerful, somewhat familiar. Michele walked along the vivid orange-yellow road and through orange brush and flaming red trees with purple shading. She strayed from the road and strolled across lush fields beyond a deserted farm and ramshackle barn in the middle of untilled land to a secret location awaiting her in the woods.

Marco told Michele they should leave, which returned her to present time and space.

***

Tuesday afternoon, Mazurek and the bouncers drove away with old furniture for the Salvation Army cleared from the rooms Dante gave to Michele. Silence prevailed. His home had returned to its natural quiet state, and he left Michele to organize her bedroom and study, where the oversize desk and chair fit with little space to spare.

Dante changed clothes, poured a scotch on the rocks, and went to his third-floor studio. He sat on the couch to collect his thoughts. He had known Michele for less than twenty-four hours, yet sensed an indefinable bond between them beyond any legal guardianship. Was it a psychic thing similar to what he had with her Aunt Madeleine? No, it was something deeper, which had yet to be made clear.

Dante began to paint a profile of Michele in a stylized sixteenth-century dress and a headdress that flowed into an arch with receding arches in the background. He chose Milanese colors: sienna, greens, plus some black, vermilion, pink, and flesh tones for Michele's face.

***

Michele sat at her desk and stared into the brass bowl. The house was calm and tranquil enough for Mié to come out of hiding. She joined Goji on the desk as Michele translated several quatrains into English for Dante, as she had promised. One caused her to write an archaic series of glyphs in her journal how pleased she was to learn they would be entwined throughout eternity.

Michele read another quatrain but did not translate. She stared again into the bowl. *"Dedans le blanc ... les enfants transportés ... moi aussi ... tout captifs* .... They are near. They are coming for me. Men in white... now I cannot see. Why can I not see?"

***

Dante went downstairs when the doorbell rang. He'd given Michele instructions never to open the door. Conlon entered and gave Dante the five copies he requested of Madeleine's death certificates.

"You can bury her whenever you claim the body. How's Michele coping?"

"Can't say. She doesn't show her emotions."

Michele came from the kitchen and invited Marco and Doyle to the dining room for coffee and sweet rolls. There, she announced her firm intention to attend school the following day. Dante agreed it would help distract Michele from grieving over her aunt's death.

About ten minutes later, they heard sirens. Dante told Michele to stay in the house. He and Conlon hurried to the street. Squad cars blocked an ambulance parked next door. Police moved citizens back, and inspectors from the local precinct began interviewing witnesses, the majority being elementary school age children who had been on their way home from school.

The front window of the ambulance had been smashed and its metal roof ripped open as if made of paper. Two men sat in the front seats, shredded and exsanguinated.

Several eyewitnesses said a rock crashed into the window; others insisted it was a large bird. Conlon knew one thing for certain. He told Dante Joy McClellan and the Jon Doe had been mutilated the same way, except the girl survived.

Uniformed officers went to the neighboring houses to inquire if anyone had seen anything unusual on the street. Dante and Conlon never heard the ambulance's siren. Neither had anyone else.

"Go back inside, Marco. This is police business. I'll call you sometime tomorrow."

***

Dressed in a royal purple gold trimmed robe in a vast reception hall, The Woman sat on a throne chair. Several dozen minions trembled. She glared at Security and in a rant that reddened her face rebuked him for failing. The Woman further chastised Security for choosing two fools who were supposed to abduct the girl late at night after the fog rolled in and the streets were empty instead of broad daylight in front of witnesses.

Security groveled. "The police will suppress everything to avoid panicking the City.

"Of course they will. I have arranged that already with the top echelons at SFPD, the newspapers, and all radio stations. Now, tell me. What did you see?"

Security blamed the men for leaving before he gave the okay, and he chased after them. The moment they parked the ambulance, something not human smashed into the front window, burst out from the roof, and disappeared all in a blur, leaving both men bloody and minced.

"Not human? Describe it."

"I can't. It happened too fast."

The Woman leaned back in the chair and cursed in a language Security did not understand. "Have you a new plan that can succeed without going near the girl's home?"

"I have."

THE SORCERESS AND THE SKULL

The woman listened and approved Security's proposal. "Beware. My patience is exhausted. I promise you this, I shall not tolerate another failure. You are not indispensable."

CHAPTER 16
ASH WEDNESDAY

After Dante drove Michele to Lowell, he spent the better part of the morning with his lawyers, to whom he gave three copies of Madeleine's death certificate: one for the probate judge, one for the magistrate who would give him power of attorney, and a third for the funeral home. Michele had asked him to honor her aunt's wish for cremation with no ceremony.

Next, Dante brought a death certificate to Michele's bank. From there he met Conlon for lunch at Original Joe's on Union near Stockton. A devout Catholic, Doyle had a cross of ashes on his forehead.

They ordered their usual Joe's Special: eggs scrambled with garlic, spinach, and ground beef, and wine for Dante alone. Conlon gave up alcohol for Lent and settled for a Pepsi. "One way to lose a bit of girth, Marco." He paused and scowled. "Bastards."

"Who?"

"Those diners staring at your face."

"I'm used to it, Doyle."

"Don't be offended, Marco, but maybe some plastic surgeon can help. I read somewhere they've got new techniques developed since the war."

Dante changed the subject. "Anything you can tell me about the ambulance and the two victims?"

Conlon told Dante it had no gurney, but they found a bottle of chloroform, duct tape, other restraints, and a sack large enough to hold a small boy or girl. None of the victims carried IDs. No evidence the ambulance came from any known hospital or clinic.

Dante reminded Conlon of a line from Madeleine's quatrains, "... the greatest daughter taken."

"Yes, it does seem they came to kidnap Michele."

"No other reason for them being there, Doyle."

"How will you keep the girl safe? We can't give you police protection."

"I have my Army .45 and a carbine, but I can't lock Michele at home day and night. She begged me to take her to school. I thought it best to get her out of the house so she can be distracted from mourning her aunt. I drove Michele to Lowell. I've already alerted the administration and each of her teachers that I am the only adult who may have contact with Michele during school hours."

"I hope that will be enough"

***

Michele's nemesis Joy McClellan, was hospitalized. Joy's clique of girls no longer made derisive comments or any physical contact. Instead, each avoided eye contact and backed away in fear whenever Michele approached. She had keen hearing and overheard whispers about "that menacing looking man" who had accompanied her the previous day. No one had the courage to ask Michele who he might be.

After the bell rang, ending the last morning class, students dispersed to different parts of the campus: cafeteria, the concrete area between the main building and the gym, which had outdoor basketball courts where boys played three-on-three or shot free throw elimination for quarters. Groups of girls sat in the cafeteria and outside on benches gossiping.

Boys had permission to leave campus during lunch. Some purchased sandwiches and quarts of milk at a market across the street from Ashbury on Hayes. Others found places where they could smoke. Girls could not leave the school grounds. The wooded Golden Gate Park Panhandle was a block away from Lowell along Fell Street. To encourage more boys to stay on campus during lunch, the school administration allowed pop tunes to be played through loudspeakers in the open air Quad for dancing and listening.

Michele went to her hall locker. She put on a camel hair overcoat over her cashmere cardigan, and like most girls at Lowell, she tied a babushka scarf at her neck. She removed a thermos filled with *potage Saint-Germain,* seasoned pea soup. It was a perfect choice on a cold and blustery day. Michele drank her soup on a bench in the Quad watching couples dance despite the weather. Two faculty members, both unmarried older women, made sure they did not move too close.

Michele finished her soup and went to the library. She browsed among the stacks. One section had all previous Lowell Yearbooks. Michele found one from the class of June 1936, the semester she guessed Marco graduated. She had never seen a photo of the way he looked before his facial injuries. What Michele found saddened her. Marco had been so handsome then.

**

Early in the afternoon, Dante set a new canvas on the easel. Mié stretched out on the couch watching each movement he made. Goji lurked at will. After an hour, Dante did not remember sketching a charcoal outline of Sandrine as the Winter Blonde for his next oil. By then it was time to bring Michele home from school.

Outside along the street, inspectors from the local precinct continued to interview neighbors regarding the two dead men in the bogus ambulance.

**

Upon their return home, Michele went to her second-floor suite and Dante to his third-floor studio. Mié again took command of the couch. Dante assumed Goji was with Michele. At 4:30, she left coffee, a sweet roll, and a note on a tray in the studio without disturbing him.

Although his house was quiet, Dante heard the melancholy sound of foghorns. He looked out the window and saw the Golden Gate Bridge immersed in a thick mist coming from the ocean. Everyone remarked how the fog had been heavier than usual and depressing of late.

Later in the evening, Dante stepped back from the easel after completing the new Winter Blonde portrait. Wrapped in an ermine coat, Sandrine stood in a glacial maw of dentated stalactites and stalagmites. She faced the viewer with a malevolent mien. Dante could not remember how he'd created realistic translucent ice and thick white fur that begged to be touched. Something compelled him to add a suggestion of madness to Sandrine's eyes and mouth. Mié meowed approval.

Michele's note reminded Dante dinner would be served at nine. He looked at his watch. 8:45. Enough time to wash.

***

Michele rang a small crystal bell as Dante entered the dining room illuminated by candles in low silver candelabras. She had placed on a white linen tablecloth his parents' formal porcelain plates, silverware and crystal stemware. Michele also selected a Burgundy from the wine cellar, which she had opened and set in a silver basket. She included a wine glass at her place setting to Dante's right. He questioned Michele about drinking wine at her age, and she said half a glass mixed with water was what Madeleine had allowed.

Mié settled Goji atop a mahogany sideboard.

Michele served a classic French onion soup, followed by scalloped potatoes and a *faux boeuf bourguignon* with ground round instead of boneless beef chunks in an amazing sauce. She offered to make dinner every evening. The play of candlelight against Michele's face and her total command of the setting and dinner made her appear much older than thirteen.

Throughout the meal, Michele answered Dante's questions. She liked Lowell and coeducation, but looked forward to attending a university in the fall. Michele planned to major in Archaeology and Ancient Languages. She had a choice of the two best universities in the Bay Area, Cal or Stanford. Perhaps later she might choose Harvard graduate school or another in Europe.

Michele informed Dante that Principal Stephens invited a recruiter from Stanford to speak with her after Easter

Vacation. Dante preferred she matriculate at his *alma mater* Cal, which would be an easier commute. If Michele chose Stanford, they'd have to move down the Peninsula.

After dinner, Michele brought coffee into the den and poured Dante a cognac. Mié and Goji watched them from the fireplace mantel. She mentioned having seen his graduation yearbook in the school library.

Dante believed he had adjusted well to his damaged face and did not want to remember how he'd looked before the war.

Michele did not pursue the subject of Dante's face, but during an earlier conversation with Doyle at lunch today, his friend had done exactly that.

CHAPTER 17
DR. PERRY GODFREY

Thursday morning as Dante dressed, he found the business card Cheryl Hale gave him; She had praised the plastic surgeon who transformed her face as best in the world. After Dante left Michele at Lowell, he drove to Dr. Godfrey's office on Van Ness and California at the eastern edge of Pacific Heights. The surgeon had a large corner suite on the top floor of a gray stone seven-story building.

No patients sat in the comfortable waiting room. Avant-garde atonal music played through a loudspeaker. Dante reacted to the nurse receptionist with both astonishment and curiosity. Not a redhead but a brunette, Miss Morgan, RN, as the desk plaque identified her, had a face identical to Cheryl Hale.

Dante introduced himself and asked for a consultation appointment.

Miss Morgan looked at her appointment ledger. "May I ask who recommended the doctor?"

"One of your patients, Cheryl Hale, gave me Dr.

Godfrey's card."

Miss Morgan left the desk and opened a door. "We have been expecting you."

Dante did not question why as she led him down a long, quiet corridor between closed rooms into Dr. Godfrey's plush, expansive office with a view northward down Van Ness to Fort Mason and the Bay. Medical books and journals filled a bookcase.

Dante faced a fit, handsome, graying man with a broken nose bent to one side. Strange, the plastic surgeon never had it repaired.

Godfrey scrutinized Dante's face. "Interesting. War injuries?"

"The surgeons at Letterman Army Hospital said they had done everything possible for me,"

"Did you bring a photo of how you looked before?"

Dante gave Godfrey the one he had taken for the Cal yearbook during his senior year.

"I believe I can accomplish what you want, but it will take several operations of more skin grafting and adding a prosthetic here and there." Godfrey removed from his cabinet a head consisting of small jigsaw puzzle pieces. "This is an invention of mine. I believe there are twelve basic facial types, based on racial and ethnic tribal characteristics, excluding certain anomalies, such as humans who resemble animals and deformities caused by trauma at birth."

Godfrey manipulated pieces on the head and added putty. "Now watch. A slight variation and here you are... or were."

Dante stared amazed at his former face. "Uncanny."

"Yours is a most challenging case. You will require multiple operations over a period of several years. I have a clinic in a quiet secluded environment where my patients can recover in comfort."

"Cheryl Hale who recommended you, and Miss Morgan, why do they have identical faces?"

Godfrey again moved pieces on the head without putty to create a model for the two women. "It is my most requested look, but true beauty must come from within. That, I cannot reproduce."

***

Thursday afternoon, Mié shrieked in the studio, and Goji materialized on the sofa beside her. Dante felt a blow to his body and almost dropped palette and brush. He checked the time. Close to two in the afternoon. Still half an hour left to finish painting his portrait of the Winter Blonde before he brought Michele home from school.

The phone rang. Conlon was calling from Lowell. Two men with false police IDs snatched Michele from her classroom. Lowell alumni D.A. Pat Brown, several members of the Police Commission, new Chief Getchell, and Conlon's police captain father were on the scene.

"Marco, there's nothing you can do at Lowell except be in the way. I promise. I'll update you later."

Shaken by Conlon's call, Dante went to the den, poured a scotch on the rocks and lit his pipe. He could not sit still and went upstairs to Michele's suite. Atop her desk lay a feather quill, inkwell, and a dictionary-size volume. A blotter divided blank pages from those with writing in no recognizable alphabet, glyph, or rune.

Mié watched Dante try each drawer at Michele's desk. All locked. No key in sight. Where was Goji? On bent knees, Dante swept his hands across the bottom of the desk hoping Michele taped her key to the wood. She hadn't. When he stood, Goji was on the desk, a key at his feet.

Dante unlocked each drawer and discovered a treasure trove of information in addition to the quatrains. He held a half dozen international passports each for Michele and Madeleine under different names. Passbooks from banks in the USA, France, England, Switzerland, and Canada showed the extent of Michele's liquid wealth. Dante found lists of stocks, bonds, and real estate holdings throughout the world. Other records revealed sequestered stockpiles of gold, silver and precious gems.

Dante next opened an envelope containing more than thirty quatrains and a note Michele left for him:

> Marco,
> I have begun to translate the quatrains as you requested. I now know that I must be taken so we can have a final confrontation with The Byzantine and remove any threat from *La blond d'Hiver*. These first four quatrains contain clues that will reveal where I am. I know we shall prevail in the end.
> Michele
> p.s. Do not trust Sandrine. Never let her read my quatrains.

***

Thursday afternoon The Woman faced a one-way mirror and watched Michele fall into a medically induced sleep. Difficult to believe the girl was thirteen. Her figure was that of a ten-year-old.

Yes, she now had Michele but was furious at the blundering fools for taking the girl from a classroom full of witnesses who could describe them to a police sketch artist. It was the pinnacle of stupidity. Worse, the abduction led the news on every radio station in the Bay Area and late editions of the afternoon newspapers.

Security defended his plan. He reminded The Woman that three of his men had died under suspicious circumstances. They had no other alternative. The Woman countered with an order for Security to liquidate his clumsy underlings.

The Endocrinologist approached with the results of Michele's physical. He described the norms for female puberty and the degree to which Michele conformed to standard physiological and anatomical evidence of menarche. Thirteen was the median age for the first bleeding cycle with an average of seventeen percent body fat. Michele had less than five percent. Once the lab results showed the condition of her hypothalamus, secretions of estrogen, and hormone levels, he would begin the injections. Depending upon Michele's reaction to the serum, favorable results should appear in a week or two.

"Can it be done in less than a week, perhaps two or three days?"

"Surely you do not want me to risk the girl's life with mega doses. Children have died during such experiments or had their minds destroyed."

The Woman considered her options. One choice was viable. She would have to leave the country with Michele sooner than intended. Security's original plan to kill *Le Crâne* when they took the girl was another fiasco. As Michele's guardian, *Le Crâne* would possess a significant number of unpublished quatrains that the abductors should have brought with the girl. *Le Crâne* and *La blond d'Hiver* might learn from them where Michele had been taken before the serum worked.

"Take that risk now and give her the first injection."

***

Thursday evening the doorbell rang. Dante locked the quatrains in the desk and went downstairs.

Sandrine stood in the doorway. She held several books. "We must talk."

Sandrine arrived at a most inconvenient time. Dante expected to hear an update from Conlon at any moment about progress made in the search for Michele.

Each time Dante saw Sandrine, her physical beauty astonished him, but there was nothing beneath the surface except a cold and brilliant mind. Her aura seemed gloom-shrouded like the fog blanketing the City.

Dante mistrusted the Winter Blonde but wanted to hear what she had to say. He invited Sandrine to sit in the den. Mié hissed at her from the fireplace mantel next to Goji, whose body pulsated. Sandrine ignored the cat and told Dante she heard about the abduction of a high school girl listening to the radio. She supposed Michele was the victim and came to help search for the girl.

Sandrine recited verbatim the quatrain Madeleine had read to them. It predicted *Le Crâne* and *La blond d'Hiver* would be allies against The Byzantine. Sandrine asked to read and translate all quatrains in the envelope now in Dante's possession because they might reveal where Michele has been taken. That was why she brought the books. They described how Nostradamus obfuscated his prophecies.

Michele's note had ended with *Do not trust Sandrine. Never let her read my quatrains.* Dante had his own reasons for allowing Sandrine to get her hands on those verses. He doubted she'd give him an honest translation from the French. His instincts convinced him both *La blond d'Hiver* and The Byzantine coveted Michele and the prophecies for reasons he had yet to discover.

When Dante told Sandrine the quatrains were not available, she did not ask where they might be, nor was she confrontational. Sandrine must have known he had lied about the prophecies. What critical information was the Winter Blonde keeping from him? He did not need any quatrain to predict they would be adversaries.

Sandrine described her encounter with the peculiar man at the bookstore near where Warwick disappeared, his belief in British-Israel Truth, and the Society of the Ten.

She showed Dante her invitation. "Tomorrow night the Society is having their annual gala, to which, as a racially pure *Überfraülein*, I have been invited. If I can learn more about them, I might be able to find out what happened to Warwick and if his disappearance is somehow connected to Michele's abduction, which I now believe is likely."

Dante memorized the Hillsborough address. "You may be right. Then I'll go with you."

"You would never be allowed entry. The Society's members are so racist they view Italians to be the same as being colored."

"What time do you have to be there?"

"Seven-thirty for the reception."

The phone rang. It was Doyle.

"Marco, they want you downtown, now."

CHAPTER 18
INTERVIEW

Dante had met many ranking officers through Doyle over the years but not any of the men who sat opposite him at a conference table Thursday night the three strangers included a Police Commissioner, a Deputy Chief from the Missing Persons Unit, and the Head of the local FBI Bureau. A female stenographer sat near the table.

Where was Doyle? Why weren't his father, Chief Getchell, or any of the Lowell SFPD mafia present? Why had they brought in the FBI so soon?

Dante became defiant under their hostile scrutiny. "What progress is being made in the search for Michele?"

He did not believe the Commissioner who told him everything possible was being done to find the girl.

The Deputy Chief held a piece of paper. "We have Inspector Sergeant Doyle Conlon's statements. Tell us how you met Madeleine Desaix and her niece Michele."

Dante described his being compelled to sketch Madeleine's face, their meeting at Serafino's gallery, and the night of her death.

The Deputy Chief made check marks on Doyle's report as Dante spoke. "Tell us why Mrs. Desaix would make you, a total stranger, executor, and trustee of the girl's estate?"

Dante showed them the quatrain Madeleine had read to him and Sandrine. "Both aunt and niece claimed to be descendants of Nostradamus. I don't know if any of you can read French. I can't. But, look at my face. She said I was *Le Crâne,* which translates as the Skull. He, as predicted, would rescue Michele from someone known as The Byzantine and as *Verbedieu,* Word of God."

The FBI agent held the quatrain. "Do *you* believe the girl is descended from Nostradamus?"

"It doesn't matter what I believe. The people who took Michele believe she is and that she will have all the Seer's gifts of precognition after she enters puberty."

The FBI agent leaned forward. "Who is *La blond d'Hiver?*"

"It translates as the Winter Blonde." Dante gave him Sandrine's name and position at Cal. "May I have the quatrain? It's not mine to give away. It is part of Michele's estate."

The agent held on to the paper. "Are there more?"

"None that I have found. Again I ask. What are you doing to find Michele?"

The Deputy Chief confronted Dante. "We have more questions. What do you know about the mutilation of Joy McClellan and the murders of three other men in cases Inspector Conlon is working on?"

"He's the investigator, not me. Ask him."

"Then listen to me and heed all I say, Mr. Dante. Leave the search for Michele Desaix to the police and FBI. Do not go looking for her on your own. And do not involve Inspector Conlon."

Dante stood and snatched the quatrain from the FBI agent. "I have nothing more to say. Any further questioning will be in the presence of my attorneys."

He left the conference room perplexed why they had been so hostile. To hell with their threats. He'd begin his own search for Michele and involve Doyle as he saw fit.

***

Early Friday in the AM, Dante arrived home from the interrogation in a foul mood. So was Mié. The cat greeted him with short angry meows and led the way into the kitchen. Her food and water bowls were empty. Dante compensated Mié with a can of tuna for humans and half a dozen ice cubes, which she liked to lick and then sweep across the floor in a feline version of soccer.

In the den, Dante poured a cognac. He could not relax even though he was exhausted from what had been happening since Monday in his parallel world from the moment he awakened to the hostile interview at SFPD. He went upstairs to Michele's desk. Goji stood at one end. Was it his imagination or had the chimera grown in height?

Dante stood at the brass bowl and tripod. Michele had emptied the water, burned the laurel branch, and polished the brass. Tuesday when she moved from her home, she asked Rafe to transplant a laurel tree in Dante's back yard and bring several gallons of pure well water for the bowl.

Glyphs similar to what Dante had seen in the journal had been etched on the outside and inside of the bowl except for the interior bottom, which was mirror clear. He peered into the bowl and saw his distorted reflection.

Sipping cognac, Dante read Michele's translations of four quatrains. They told a coherent story of conflict with The

Byzantine but offered no clues to where she had been taken. He would have to find someone he trusted to translate the other two dozen verses. Dante opened Michele's journal again confounded by the glyphs. From what ancient civilization had they come? He had a dizzy spell as the markings began to move and form odd three-dimensional shapes.

CHAPTER 19
SYNAPTIC CONNECTIONS

Daybreak Friday morning, Dante awakened in the studio standing over his sketchpad on a table adjacent to the easel. He remembered nothing after he opened Michele's peculiar journal, not even sketching on a fresh pad these outlines of her full face and two profiles. Dante had delineated Michele's imploring eyes.

In another more realistic sketch, a physician with a syringe stood over Michele, who seemed to be in twilight sleep.

Dante had outlined in charcoal on a different page corridors in glaring white chalk. All sketches were of interiors. Dante doubted Michele could him a specific location. Her abductors would have blindfolded or drugged her. Most likely, they brought Michele to a private clinic located somewhere in the Bay Area, in the City, Marin County, around Berkeley, or down the Peninsula.

These sketches he did not remember drawing convinced Dante that Michele had the same ability as her aunt to communicate with him. Unlike his previous experience with Madeleine, he hoped to receive more thought transmissions from Michele.

Dante opened a blank page in the sketchpad and tried to open his mind. "Michele, contact me again. Tell me ... you must tell me where you are."

***

After a shave and a long refreshing shower, Dante found a note from Conlon on the foyer floor dropped through the mail slot on his front door. Doyle asked for a meeting on the beach at the far end of the Sunset District south of Golden Gate Park with a caveat: Do not phone me.

The day was bright and clear, temperature in the low fifties with a typical San Francisco gusty wind chill that stung Dante's sensitive face and knifed through his clothes. Conlon arrived resembling an angry grizzly. He scanned the beach, parking area, and homes across the road before he said a word. "Just checking to make sure they aren't watching us."

At the shoreline, Conlon told Dante his phone at SFPD was being tapped. He believed his apartment had been bugged too. His face clouded when he described how the FBI took control of the search for Michele within the hour after she was abducted. The new Bureau Chief, Gordon Wark, had been meddling in police matters since his arrival the previous December colluding with the same Deputy Chief and Police Commissioner, who questioned Dante.

Conlon removed an envelope from his jacket inside pocket. "Do you trust Sandrine?"

"No."

Conlon handed Dante the envelope. "This may help explain why you should not trust her. I called in a favor, and

101

my contact at Cal brought me this copy of her résumé."

Sandrine had so astronomical an IQ, at age five unnamed parents placed the girl in a special environment to nurture her genius. A group of behavioral psychologists ran the controversial boarding school located in Geneva, Switzerland. They developed the intellect of children in their care without emotional nurturing. Sandrine earned her first M.A. at sixteen and before age twenty accumulated PhDs from prestigious European universities. She also learned to play well several musical instruments.

Conlon pointed out a huge gap in Sandrine's CV: no evidence of where she was and what she did from 1934 until 1943, when she arrived at Cal with the highest recommendations and Warwick hired her. "Sandrine Arnoul might not be her real name, and this personal history may not be true at all."

They returned to their cars, and Dante showed Conlon his charcoals of Michele. "Doyle, look at the corridors in this sketch, and here where she's on a table. It's obvious Michele would have been taken to a private clinic."

"I agree, but which one?"

Dante described his appointment with Dr. Godfrey. "Maybe he has a list of private clinics he uses for his patients."

"Let me handle Godfrey. I am the inspector. The entire situation stinks, Marco. I promise you this. No one is going to stop me working a case that concerns my best friend even if it is not a Homicide."

Dante put the sketchpad in the trunk of his car. "We have to arrange how best to communicate without using our phones."

"We can meet each day around noon at *Pizzeria Bella Venezia* on Union or call from a pay phone and leave a message. We can trust the owners. They have known us and our families for years."

"When do we meet next?"

"Here tomorrow, one in the afternoon."

"Doyle, perhaps the unholy trio may be taking orders from The Byzantine mentioned in Madeleine's quatrains."

***

Dante had to find someone reliable to translate the quatrains. Dr. Monash was the first person who came to mind. The psychiatrist made time for him between appointments. Dante showed Monash his sketchpad and described all that happened from his last visit Monday morning to Michele's abduction and the interrogation at SFPD.

"Doctor, I am into something way over my head. I no longer have control over my life. I feel more certain I awakened on Monday in some parallel universe."

"Your compulsion to draw Mrs. Desaix and now her niece can be explained. Your head wounds may have triggered some kind of synaptic connection in the brain that has made you more receptive to another's thoughts. Stranger cases have been documented. After a head injury, one can be fluent in a language he never knew before, play with skill a musical instrument without having had lessons, or become a criminal when no such tendencies existed earlier."

Dante stood at the window and watched traffic on the sidewalks and streets around Union Square. Everything seemed normal below. "Am I crazy to believe I can find Michele through the quatrains?"

"I am fluent in French. I should be able to read those verses and then tell you what I think."

"When can I bring them to you?"

"I am booked with patients for the rest of the day and have pressing obligations tomorrow. You have my address. Be there at ten Sunday morning.

CHAPTER 20
DECIPHERING NOSTRADAMUS

Friday afternoon, Dante brewed a pot of strong coffee, fed and watered Mié. He brought his mug into the den, gathered the books Sandrine left on the couch last night, and carried them upstairs to Michele's desk. One was a biography of Nostradamus:

The Seer became a successful physician, settled in Salon-de-Provence, and served the Valois dynasty as doctor and member of the Privy Council. Ravaged by gout and arthritis, he died a painful yet prosaic death in 1566.

Those were intolerant times: the Inquisition; witch burning; French Catholics and Protestant Huguenots slaughtering each other. Nostradamus came close to being burned at the stake, which explains why he made his published prophecies ambiguous. About twelve hundred quatrains were mentioned by scholars, of which nine hundred-and-fifty survived. In his other writings, Nostradamus alluded to a larger number of verses, which were not for ordinary mortals to read.

Another book explained how the Seer obscured his predictions. The third and fourth books had differing interpretations of his prophecies, one written in the 1920s, the other published at the end of 1945.

Had Sandrine deliberately left the books yesterday evening or had she forgotten to take them with her after he received the call to appear at SFPD headquarters.

Twenty-four hours had passed since Michele's abduction. Dante's concern for her safety dominated his thoughts and actions. Panic too. Michele had not made a psychic connection since he drew those sketches of her at some clinic or hospital. He again read Michele's note. She wrote that clues to find her could be found in the unpublished quatrains. She had translated four out of more than thirty.

Dante read Michele's translations. No clues there to reveal where she had been taken. He scanned the untranslated quatrains. In several prophecies, The Byzantine was named *Verbedieu*, literally Word of God. Which word of God? The Old or New Testaments? The Koran? A person or a number of people?

One fact was certain, which Madeleine had emphasized. The Byzantine wanted Michele, and now he had her.

Dante hunted for Byzantine and *Verbedieu* in the indexes of all four books published with the complete prophecies of Nostradamus. He found twenty-one references to Byzantium, all translated in the context of war, but none for *Verbedieu, Le Crâne,* nor *La Blond d'Hiver.*

For the next several hours, Dante read, scanned, and made notes. One book made the most sense, *Deciphering Nostradamus* by Pierre Cadoux, Ph.D. published in November 1945. In clear prose, Cadoux led the reader step by step as he explained how the Seer made his verses ambiguous.

For those illiterate in French, the quatrains would have to be translated before any interpretations could be made. Although Nostradamus wrote in Medieval and/or Old French, he used a Latin syntax. Therefore, one would have to convert the original quatrains into Latin and from Latin to English to achieve a clearer meaning. Before that could happen, one needed to know what Cadoux called "Rules of the Seer."

Nostradamus created anagrams more diabolical than the mere shuffling of letters. He changed, omitted, or added them to an already scrambled word. He applied rhetorical, grammatical, and poetic techniques from Greek and Latin usage. He alluded to ancient and medieval mythology and geography, the Old and New Testaments, and the Kabbala.

During Nostradamus' lifetime, printers used many letters, such as u and v, interchangeably. Furthermore, the first publishers of the prophecies committed typographical errors reprinted for more than four hundred years.

Nostradamus often used words with different meanings in several languages. *Pont*, which appeared in many of his quatrains, was *bridge* in French. In another context, he used it to mean the sea, from the Greek *pontos*. At other times, it was a reference to the Papacy from the Latin *Pontifex*.

Cadoux concluded his book with:

To achieve a flawless interpretation of Nostradamus' prophecies, one would need the services of experts in the diverse fields of occult and relevant scholarship, astrology and guileful cryptanalysis, or be a polymath in all languages and ambiguities used by the Seer.

THE SORCERESS AND THE SKULL

Sandrine came to Dante's mind. She had all the language skills required to make an accurate translation of the quatrains, but did *La Blond d'Hiver* have the ability to interpret them? Dante experimented with Byzantine, playing by the Seer's rules. It might be one person or a symbolic name. The press and politicians described Stalin and the Kremlin as Byzantine.

Dante created an anagram from Byzantine, *By Ten Nazis.*

Fascination with the prophecies of Nostradamus had continued throughout the centuries because after the fact several of his prophecies proved to be accurate. Royalty and national leaders from Henry II and Catherine de Medici through Empress Josephine to Hitler and Goebbels believed Nostradamus could see the future. During the recent World War, both Allies and Nazis used his quatrains to prove each side was certain to win as part of their propaganda.

Cadoux ridiculed authors who believed Nostradamus had predicted Hitler. A quatrain, number 24 of his Century II, was a typical example of after-the-fact proof he could see the future. In this case, the word *Hister* was cited as evidence he foresaw Hitler.

Dante read Cadoux's translation:

> *Betes farouches de faim flueves tranner:*
> *Plus part du champ encontre Hister sera,*
> *En cage de fer le grand fera trainer,*
> *Quand rien enfant de Germain observera.*

> Beasts ferocious from hunger will swim across rivers:
> The greater part of the region will be against the
>   Hister,
> The great one will cause it to be dragged in an iron

cage,
When the German's child will observe nothing.

The verse was meaningless to Dante even if he substituted Hitler for Hister. Yet he understood why some would want to believe Nostradamus foretold something about *Der Führer* because the word German appeared in the quatrain, and *rien,* the French word for *nothing,* could be the Rhine. Cadoux asserted Hister was Ister, the Latin word for the Danube.

Dante referred to the title page of the unpublished prophecies. *Le Crâne* could be a literal reference to a skull; a member of the exclusive Yale Society, Skull and Bones; a classical or Biblical allusion; or an anagram for flesh, *carne.*

According to Cadoux, when Nostradamus used a specific date in his prophecies, the basis of the count was uncertain. Was it based on the Christian calendar? If so, was it dated from the Nativity or physical death of Christ, the Council of Nicea in 365 AD, the year of his own birth or death?

Cadoux stated that Nostradamus seldom used specific dates, which is why the year 1999 fascinated all who read his quatrains.

L'an mil neuf cens nonante neuf sept mois
Du ciel Viendra un grand Roi d'effrayeur;
Resuciter le grand Roi d'Angolmois,
Avant apres Mars regner par bonheur.

This quatrain in translation described a great King of Terror bursting from the sky in the seventh month of the year 1999 and resurrecting a great Mongol King, *Angolmois* being the accepted anagram for *Mongolois* or Mongols, while Mars reigned supreme over a good or just war.

Cadoux wrote that *Sept,* the seventh month, could be either July or September, depending whether Nostradamus used the Julian or Gregorian calendar. He added that 1999 AD should not be taken at face value, and instead the month and year had to be one of the Seer's deceptions. Cadoux believed this quatrain described a surprise aerial attack coming from an evil Islamic Fundamentalist Empire, thus initiating the final conflict against The Third Antichrist.

Cadoux extracted *Islam* from *Angolmois* and suggested Nostradamus did not intend for 1999 to represent a specific year; it was a reference to the Beast of the Apocalypse. Cadoux advised the reader to remove the first digit and invert the three nines. The result would be 666, the Mark of the Beast as written in Revelations, 13.18.

Dante removed a Bible from Michele's bookcase and found the appropriate passage: *Here is wisdom. Let him that hath understanding count the number of the beast: for it is the number of a man; and his number is Six Hundred Three Score and Six.*

Dante decided it did not matter if Nostradamus was accurate or inaccurate, a genius or a fake. From the sixteenth century, thousands of otherwise rational individuals believed in the Seer's ability to predict the future. Catherine de Medici, as queen-regent of France, made Nostradamus a Privy Counselor and Physician-in-Ordinary as well.

Michel de Nostredame's biography was contradictory in part. He may have been born at Saint-Rémy in Provence, or somewhere else. His paternal and maternal grandfathers were either physicians to the Dukes of Provence, Lorraine, and Calabria, or they were grain dealers. Before Michel was born, his family took the de Nostredame name when they renounced their Jewish faith and converted to Catholicism rather than face exile.

DONALD MICHAEL PLATT

Dante agreed with Cadoux's conclusion. There was not enough time in any one person's life span to interpret the prophecies with unerring accuracy, unless a shortcut existed. That would be Michele, if she inherited all Nostradamus' skills of precognition.

Unaware how much time had passed and exhausted from lack of sleep, Dante passed out at Michele's desk.

CHAPTER 21
STRANGE AWAKENING

Something bumped Dante's shoulder. He opened one eye. The side of his head lay atop Michele's desk where he'd fallen asleep among books and notes. It was Saturday, nine in the morning, and now Mié was in his face.

The sound of bubbling caused Dante to rise and stand over the brass bowl. How did it become filled with water, and who placed the laurel branch in it? Goji? The inert Chimera was on the desk edge beside it.

Dante left the chair and stood over the bowl. The turbulence stopped, and the water became mirror clear. He saw a hard man with cruel lines around his mouth.

"Is he The Byzantine, Goji?"

When the image disappeared, Dante hurried upstairs to the studio, found his sketchpad, and drew in pencil what he remembered of the man's face. He returned to Michele's suite.

Mié made her usual *feed me now* demanding sounds. Dante accommodated her in the kitchen and ate a light breakfast. He then performed his morning ablutions and read the notes from last night.

Back in the studio, Dante began a new portrait. Mié and Goji watched him from the table near the easel. The Abyssinian did not move from her Egyptian goddess pose or blink, and Goji's eyes expressed similar inscrutability. Dante added both to his new *Little Sorceress* painting of Michele. The doorbell rang.

***

Conlon brushed past Dante, with a flamboyant celebrity known as the Psychic to the Famous, Horatio Lefton, in tow.

Seated in the den Lefton closed his eyes. "Something happened outside near where I parked on the street. Two men in an ambulance, murdered."

"No, Marco, I told him nothing about it. Do you see the killer, Horatio?"

"Yes. Doyle. Improbable as it may be, the killer was a green gargoyle."

Short, plump and pink-skinned as a cherub, Lefton wore a purple cashmere jacket with a heliotrope boutonnière, vermilion Ascot, and yellow silk shirt matching his trousers, socks, and shoes. A jeweled golden ring on one of his pudgy fingers was emblazoned with the sign of Aquarius.

At the time Dante recovered from his wounds in Hawaii, Doyle sent letters describing how he and Lefton worked together to solve several difficult cases.

Dante saw Conlon staring at him with a police inspector's classic fish eye. Dante guessed what Doyle must have been thinking. Conlon had seen the malachite figurine, but after what Lefton said, would Doyle believe Goji was capable of independent action?

Dante had become accustomed to the inexplicable, and

Doyle worked with a psychic. How might Lefton react to Goji? No sign of the chimera downstairs, but Mié followed everyone into Michele's suite and leaped onto the fireplace mantel.

"No, don't bother opening the drapes." Lefton touched each volume along one of the shelves. "Amazing library. I'd almost sell my soul to possess it. This book on the desk. May I open it?"

Dante nodded yes,

Lefton gasped when he saw the glyphs. "Do you know what this is?"

"Some form of ancient writing." Dante heard a gurgling sound. Water in the brass bowl rippled. He felt a painful prick on his arm, and the water became still.

Lefton stood beside Dante. "You saw and experienced something, but don't tell me what. I want to experience it myself. This room is alive with so many presences and images, I...." He dropped to his knees on the rug in front of the desk and traced the same patterns of the Kabbala the same as Sandrine the night Mrs. Desaix died. "I thought so. All of a piece."

Lefton sat at the desk and placed both palms on its surface. He rocked back and forth as if in prayer for close to a minute. "There has been a death at this desk, a recent death but in a different house. A woman. Heart attack. There is much age in this room, furniture and objects centuries old, and too many images. Don't have to be a psychic for that."

Lefton again rocked and closed his eyes. "Odd. I see a man. He has a beard. He is sitting at this same desk. His clothes, they are not contemporary. Yes, the brass bowl is there. Same Abyssinian on the mantel, not alive, but as a statuette of an Egyptian cat deity. Where is the green gargoyle? It should be on the desk."

Dante showed Lefton the quatrains. "These were in the lower drawer."

Lefton closed his eyes and ran his fingers over each page. "I see the woman again, and a blonde, beautiful but cold, calculating. Beware of her."

Dante rubbed his arm where he felt the prick. Where the hell was Goji? "Can you see anything in the bowl?"

"Nothing, it is refusing to let me in. I'm sorry, Marco."

"There's another room you must see."

The moment they entered Michele's bedroom, Lefton closed his eyes and rocked again. "A girl's room. A pretty child, a tiny brunette. She was abducted by two men from a school classroom."

"Can you describe them?"

"I cannot see their faces."

"The car, a license plate?"

"An ambulance... gone."

Lefton's vision confirmed Dante's belief Michele had been taken to a private clinic or hospital. "Where have they taken her?"

"I cannot see." After long moments, Lefton opened his eyes. "I did not learn the girl's connection to you, Marco."

"The woman who died appointed me Michele's guardian. They claim descent from Nostradamus."

"Nostradamus? Of course. He is the man I saw at the desk. That explains everything. It is no claim. They *are* descendants of Nostradamus. May I see your studio?"

Upstairs in his studio, Dante's charcoal sketches of Madeleine and Michele held Lefton's interest. "So unlike your cheerful impastos of San Francisco. Your unfinished portrait of the girl, that gargoyle is the same I saw in my vision. It is hiding from me but very near. This man in your pencil sketch, he is not The Byzantine."

115

Dante gaped at Lefton. He had not spoken that name to the psychic. "Who is he?"

"Someone capable of ultimate evil."

Lefton focused on Dante's portrait of Sandrine in an icy maw. "Nothing more for me to accomplish here. I may be able to help in another way if you come to my home."

Conlon glanced at his watch. "Not now. I have to work my other cases. Marco. follow Horatio and leave a message for me after you're through. I'll check in later. Forgot to mention I went to Dr. Godfrey's office on Van Ness. It was gutted of furniture and files. Management said he paid off his lease but left no forwarding address. One more thing. I want to have a serious talk with you about Goji later this evening."

CHAPTER 22
JUDICIAL ASTROLOGY

Situated between 26th and 27th Avenues where they ended on Sea Cliff Avenue, Lefton's off-white, blue-trimmed art deco home had rounded edges, portholes on the sides, and curved balconies, with a large bay window facing the Golden Gate Bridge and Marin County beyond.

Inside, Lefton handed Dante the charcoal and pastel sketch of Madeleine he had given Dr. Monash. "I believe this belongs to you. Marco, you should know that Laurence and I consult with each other regarding his patients and my clients."

"Did the two of you come up with anything to help me find Michele?"

"Come with me."

Dante followed the psychic into his second-floor office. Drawn black drapes blocked what would have been a clear view of the Bay. Diplomas and roll-down astrological charts hung on the walls between metal file cabinets. Books, manuscripts, and papers cluttered Lefton's curved rosewood

THE SORCERESS AND THE SKULL

desk.

Dante sat opposite the psychic. "Doyle told me you're an astrologer."

"Judicial astrologer. What the stars reveal supplements my psychic gifts. Knowing the birth sign of a victim has been an important aid to my seeing what happened at a crime site. If you will allow me to cast the girl's horoscope, the zodiac may reveal where she has been taken. Do you know her date of birth?"

"December 21, 1932."

"Location?"

"St. Remy, France."

"Hour and minute?"

"Don't know."

Lefton opened a book, scanned a few pages and wrote on a sheet of paper. "I sense the girl, Michele, may have been born on the same day, place, and instant as her ancestor Nostradamus. Let me see what I can do with that." Lefton calculated and frowned. "I need more information. Well, your horoscope should be sufficient. I may discover who is in conflict with you and the girl. Before we begin, I must know the extent of your previous experiences with astrologers."

"I sometimes read my horoscope in the newspapers for entertainment."

"And as entertainment, they are useless solar horoscopes based on the position of the sun on the day of one's birth. They ignore the minute details of precise locations of each planet and significant stars at the instant of birth."

"I expected you to be more thorough."

"And scientific." Lefton pointed to a cluster of framed diplomas on the wall behind him. "I have a Doctorate in Mathematics from the University of London, another in Astronomy from the University of Utrecht, and a third in

Psychology from Vienna. That large plaque is my diploma from the London Faculty of Astrological Studies. There, one must complete a rigid two year course of study, and then work with clients under a strict code of ethics."

"I am impressed, surprised too. Now I understand why, given your résumé, you are sought by so many people of influence."

"But rejected by men of science. The sterile logic of the scientific mind is no match for true psychic abilities."

"As with Nostradamus?"

"Perhaps. Genius, the ultimate exception, always triumphs over accepted norms." Lefton selected a pencil. "And now, I shall construct your genethlical horoscope."

"Genethlical?"

"Your natal, individual horoscope. I need your full name, precise instant of birth, if possible, and exact location. I prefer you write it down. The instant of birth is crucial to casting an accurate horoscope." He pushed paper and pen at Dante.

"I do know the exact minute of my birth. One of my cousins born the same day used to needle me she was five minutes older."

Lefton read what Dante wrote and marked symbols on a chart. "I would prefer to have the exact second as well. San Francisco is not a precise enough location. Can you give me the street coordinates of the hospital where you were delivered?"

"No hospital. No time for it. My mother gave birth to me at home on Chestnut near Kearny." Dante gave Lefton the address. "Does knowing the second of birth and precise location matter all that much?"

"Yes. During any twenty-four hour period, there are 360 possible ascendants, each with its own mid-heaven. A

119

THE SORCERESS AND THE SKULL

different degree of the Zodiac rises above the horizon every four minutes. It is regrettable so many people who come to me cannot furnish the exact minute of birth. An error of one minute, even seconds, can affect the selection of the correct ascendant and mid-heaven. The most accurate reading is possible if we have the precise instant of birth."

Lefton opened a file drawer and took out a map of San Francisco. He found Chestnut and Kearny, worked out equations on scratch paper, and placed the answers on Dante's chart.

"I need to arrive at your ascendant sign and medium coeli, the M.C. or mid-heaven. To obtain that information, I use this ephemeris, which contains tables revealing what planet was where in the solar system at any given time, the sidereal time of your birth."

"What is sidereal time?"

"Sidereal time is measured by the stars, not by the sun. The sidereal day is a few minutes of clock time shorter than our ordinary twenty-four hour day. That discrepancy must be allowed for when calculating sidereal time of birth, which I have written on your chart as S.T."

Lefton filled in the rest of the chart with calculations, symbols, and connecting lines. He read them, made more calculations, and closed his eyes. "You are in danger. I see a beautiful woman of strange visage... eerie... face like a mask."

"A blonde?"

"No, her hair is a brilliant shade of red. And I repeat, her face resembles a mask."

Lefton's description perplexed Dante. Instead of Sandrine, the psychic had envisioned Warwick's office manager, Miss Hale, and the faces of Godfrey's receptionist and nurse. "Can you see anyone else?"

"The girl is with that woman."

"Where do you see them? Are they near?"

"Yes, near. Closer than I sensed at your house." Lefton rocked again. "There is another. Someone you must never trust. Yes, I see her now. The same ice blonde you painted. She also wants the girl."

"I can deal with her. Why did you say the man in the sketch is not The Byzantine?"

"Things like that happen to me. I cannot say more at this time. Your chart tells me you must be alert and cautious. This is a time of acute peril for you. Not a good day for traveling. I suggest you go home and stay there."

"Impossible. You know I have to find Michele."

Lefton opened his eyes. "I understand, and I wish I could be of more help. I must study your chart further. I may see more. Let me try something else." Lefton rose and took several Polaroid photos of Dante. "I want to see what I can learn about you from your aura." He waited until the photos appeared clear and sharp. "Marco, look at this."

Dante stood behind Lefton and saw his head and upper torso surrounded by an intense light, in which he could make out abstract forms suggesting objects and human shapes. "What does all this mean?"

"I repeat, today is not a good day for traveling. I see danger, violence in your aura. Be careful when you drive home, and you must stay there for the night. Yet, all will turn out well in the end, provided you are careful and follow your instincts. And after you find the girl, I would like to meet her. She may have psychic powers well beyond mine."

***

A heavy ocean fog had rolled in by the time Dante got into his car. He could not see much beyond the hood of his

Desoto driving a safe five miles an hour through the dense mist along Sea Cliff Avenue. He did not know he passed 26th, and instead made a right turn on 25th Avenue. A bright light covered the windshield, and for a moment Dante saw water churning in a brass bowl showing Michele atop a bed in a white room attended by physicians. Her face filled the windshield, replaced by Goji, and then Mié. His cat's piercing meow alerted Dante too late. He swerved to the left and crashed into a tree at the edge of Lobos Creek.

CHAPTER 23
ISRAELITES

Saturday evening, Sandrine raced her Chevy along a winding section of road past ranches and grand homes in the western hills of San Mateo. At the crest, she swerved onto a narrow, unlit private lane and drove to a well-lit, multistory California-Spanish style estate. A young valet helped Sandrine out of her car and sat in the driver's seat. She winced when he burned rubber and screeched away.

Sandrine fussed with her draped viridian formal trimmed with gold thread and matching stole. A haughty butler took the invitation, and she followed a burgundy liveried servant to a cavernous reception hall filled with men in tuxedos, some in uniforms splashed with medals, orders, and sashes. Bejeweled women wore elegant gowns. She recognized a governor of a nearby state, several Senators, and prominent CEOs.

Remembering MacAndrew's lecture at *The House of Books*, Sandrine identified the colorful banners along the walls for each of the Ten Tribes of Israel. All the men, even those in uniform, wore an Israelite tribal coat-of-arms patch on their jackets, and each woman had a jeweled brooch to proclaim her presumed tribal origin. Sandrine's keen sense of hearing picked up interesting pieces of conversation:

"... and then, Mary Conroy explained how the President's wife is related to King George VI."

"My dear, isn't every pure Anglo-Saxon Israelite?"

"Harry Neville is an Asher, which explains his hot temper."

"Well, I want my daughter to marry a Napthali. Most millionaires come from that tribe."

Other conversations focused on a scandal affecting the Society. The guest speaker, Dr. Yoshida, had been arrested earlier in the day when he arrived at the airport. He was identified as a war criminal who performed live experiments without anesthetics on Asian civilians and Allied POWs.

Two imperious dowagers wearing diamond tiaras and chokers blocked Sandrine's progress through the hall. One blue-haired dragon, who wore a Reuben tribal brooch of rubies, sapphires, and diamonds, measured her with disapproval.

"Young woman, where is your tribal identification? What are you? Dan? Gad?"

"Dan and Benjamin." Sandrine brushed past the woman, but a parting barb from the other dowager reminded her she was at risk here as an intruder.

"Did you see the shape of her eyes, that vulgar décolletage? I'll wager there are Slavs and other mongrels in her family woodpile."

MacAndrew materialized at Sandrine's elbow. Another surprise. He was not the sniffling, basset-faced buffoon she met the other day. Tonight he was poised and sure of himself. He swept a glass of champagne from the tray of a passing servant and offered it to her.

"Miss Kent, you look absolutely stunning. I am delighted you could come."

She sipped the champagne and scrutinized MacAndrew. The patch on his tuxedo jacket was divided into four Israelite tribal coats-of-arms. "I would not have missed this for anything."

MacAndrew led Sandrine deeper into the noisy, teeming hall. Despite its superficial glitter, she sensed a dark undercurrent of menace. At times, the people around her seemed Modigliani-extended, and she recognized one woman in particular. Amidst a circle of enthralled guests, Astrid Lambert spoke to her audience with flamboyant gestures.

"Yes, she is Astrid Lambert, whose lecture you attended the other day. I might add that her title of doctor is medical, not academic." MacAndrew took Sandrine's arm. "Miss Kent, let me further impress you with the high quality of our membership. That gentleman over there is Senator Hugh Roberts of North Carolina. The lady in the blue gown speaking with him is Mrs. Reed Cox, majority stockholder of Chandler Oil."

MacAndrew escorted Sandrine toward two distinguished men and presented her to the U.S. Naval Chief of Staff, Admiral Harold Christopher, whose patch identified him as descended from the seafaring Israelite tribe of Dan, and to portly Dr. Wilfred Langley, putative successor to the current Archbishop of Canterbury. His jacket patch was decorated with the bull of Ephraim.

Langley did not release her hand. "Have you read my book, Miss Kent?"

"No, I am sorry to say I have not."

"You must read it. I have confirmed with both

documented written proof and superb illustrations what we have known to be true all along. Ancient Israelites looked exactly like the English."

"What is the proof?"

"It was so obvious, there for all of us to see throughout the centuries. Egyptian bas-reliefs reveal the identity of the true Israelites. They are portrayed with sandy colored hair, blue or hazel eyes, and finely cut aquiline noses like all Anglo-Saxons."

A servant whispered in MacAndrew's ear. He nodded and apologized to the men for taking Sandrine away. "Come with me, Miss Kent. There is someone you must meet."

***

Sandrine and MacAndrew climbed a sweeping stairway and walked along a corridor to a sitting room and library. A man stood at the fireplace. Before he turned to face her, she already had recognized William Warwick. His tuxedo jacket was embossed with the coats-of-arms of all the Ten Lost Tribes, which Sandrine thought to be a bit of scriptural overkill.

"Where are my manuscript and notes?"

"I will explain everything in good time."

"When I saw you attending a lecture on Pyramid Prophecy..."

"I did not need to hear Astrid's tiresome lecture one more time."

Warwick seated Sandrine on the sofa and poured her a fresh glass of champagne from a bottle chilling in an ice bucket. "Stuart, do you know the true identity of this lovely young woman?"

"Of course. The moment I saw her peering into the store

window, I recognized Dr. Sandrine Arnoul from your description. She is a professor in your department. Alice Kent indeed."

Warwick eyed Sandrine from head to foot. "You have never looked lovelier although and forgive me for saying it, you look as if you could use a good night's sleep."

She raised her glass. "To your obvious good health, Dr. Warwick. I suppose you are an important member of The Ten."

"I am the Society's International President."

Sandrine was not surprised. "What is the real purpose of your society?"

"I can tell you this. In the United States alone, at least thirty million Americans are descended from kings and queens of England, and from both sides of the sheets of course. We plan to awaken them so that they may claim their rightful heritage. Time is running out."

"But not all of them are racially pure enough to be accepted," MacAndrew said.

"I wondered what your position would be regarding coloreds who are descended from those same English kings and queens through their slave owners."

Warwick and MacAndrew glared at Sandrine.

"Even if you will not tell me, I' am sure it is all connected to my missing manuscript and notes and the prophecies of Nostradamus."

"You do have an impressive and inexhaustible fund of knowledge. Please, continue."

Warwick's affectation of insouciance did not impress Sandrine, who became concerned the champagne had a high alcoholic content. Already dizzy, she blinked and squinted at Warwick, who came in and out of focus. "I know you arranged Michele's abduction."

"I have always been impressed with your fine mind. I am annoyed, however, with your meddling."

Sandrine saw two Warwicks, then one, then two again more blurred. She heard herself slurring and dropped her glass. *Drugged. My fault.* Although paralyzed and semiconscious, she heard everything they said.

Warwick took Sandrine's house keys from her bag and tossed them to MacAndrew. "Go to her apartment and search for more copies of Nostradamus' unpublished prophecies."

***

The Woman went to Michele's room to see how the girl reacted to her evening double dosage of serum during twilight sleep. The Endocrinologist told The Woman Michele's heartbeat, organs and bodily functions continued to be normal. He reiterated his concerns regarding negative side effects likely to happen if he continued the injections.

The Endocrinologist showed The Woman bruises on Michele's arms spreading from veins where the hypodermic penetrated skin. Patients he had used for experiments screamed at each injection and described the serum as a fireball coursing through their bodies. He believed the girl had absorbed enough, and they would see results within a week or two without further injections.

The Woman watched the rise and fall of Michele's breathing and considered what he advised.Were the injections enough to accelerate the girl's entrance into puberty? If Michele suffered any negative side effects, she would be of no use. Better to be cautious than sorry.

"Lusser, cease the injections. Remove all monitoring tubes, and put Michele on solid food."

Freed from all attachments to her body but still in

twilight sleep, Michele mumbled in French. The Woman stood over the girl, who repeated two names: Goji, which made no sense, and *Le Crâne*, which did.

A premonition terrified The Woman. She hurried to her suite and read translations of unpublished quatrains she had stolen and murdered to possess.

CHAPTER 24
SOME DOTS TO CONNECT

Conlon arrived at the crash site and watched a truck tow Dante's Desoto. "What happened, Marco?"

"I was driving at about five miles an hour in the fog unable to see beyond the hood when a bright light filled my windshield. Not oncoming traffic. I had a vision of Michele. I swerved to the left and hit that tree. No physical injuries, but a bent front fender and grill. Fortunately, a patrol car heard my horn and the police contacted you."

Conlon did not speak and concentrated on driving Dante home through the lingering thick fog., Inside, Dante made coffee instead of offering Doyle a drink out of respect for his friend's observance of Lent.

In the den, Dante watched Conlon inspect the room. "I doubt if anyone has bugged my home. Mie would attack any intruder." So would Goji, but Dante did not want Doyle to focus on the chimera.

Dante recounted his conversation with Lefton. "In the end, he could not tell me where Michele had been taken. He did say I was in danger and warned me not to travel. I also learned much about astrology."

"Have you heard from Sandrine?"

Dante repeated what she told him about her encounter with a most peculiar man at the bookstore, MacAndrew's theory regarding the Lost Tribes of Israel, and her invitation to the Society of the Ten's gala this evening.

Conlon expressed his disdain for the Society. SFPD had a task force tracking such organizations and groups. Although the Society claimed to be Christian, its members were nothing more than typical white-race supremacists who justified their prejudices with selected out-of-context quotations from the Scriptures.

"The Ten. Doyle, I created an anagram for Byzantine. How does 'By Ten Nazis' sound?"

"It fits the membership. The Society had been anti-war and pro-Nazi before the attack on Pearl Harbor. It is financed by wealthy eccentrics. More worrisome and odd, recent pressure from on high forced SFPD to cease its surveillance of the Society. Nothing official. I learned this on the QT but not the reason why. Marco, where is the gala?"

Dante went to his desk and wrote. "I saw Sandrine's invitation. Here is the address."

"Thanks, I'm going to head down the Peninsula and take a look, fog or no fog."

***

Dante completed Michele's portrait and relaxed in the den with a cognac waiting for Conlon. Three hours later, Doyle returned, and slumped in an armchair. "Something odd was going on at that estate. The gala was still going strong. I did not see Sandrine's red Chevrolet in the parking

131

area. I showed my badge to a valet and warned him not to touch my car and again at the front door where I demanded to speak with someone in charge. One of the members of the Society came. He was in military uniform and not friendly. I described Sandrine and wanted to know if she was still there. He took me inside.

"Did you see Sandrine?"

"Marco, big guns were attending that shindig. The County Sheriff and a Congressman who represents the District said Sandrine left around eight. They reminded me I had no authority in San Mateo County. So did those three jerks who interrogated you. Yes, the Deputy Chief, FBI honcho Wark, and the Police Commissioner are members of the Society. I saw high-ranking military brass, some national politicos, a Supreme Court Justice, and the publisher of the *San Francisco Times*. That's for openers. Then, Agent Wark warned me ... no, *threatened* is a better word ... not to bother them again."

"Warned?"

"I may be paranoid, but my gut instinct told me the Society is anti-Armenian."

"More likely they are anti-everyone except those they designate as pure Israelites. Doyle, if you can, meet me at my shrink's home tomorrow at ten in the morning. He uses Lefton the same as you. Here's his address."

"I'll be there all right, and I still want to have a chat with you about your elusive gargoyle."

I never think of the future. It comes soon enough.
Albert Einstein

PART III

SECOND WEEK IN MARCH

CHAPTER 25
CAPTIVE

Sunday morning, head aching, body weak, Sandrine awakened on top of a king size bed in a plush, windowless suite with furniture and walls hospital white. Someone removed her formal dress when she had been unconscious and replaced it with pale blue flannel pajamas and slippers.

Warwick entered, smug and natty reeking of too much aftershave. A dour nurse followed with a cart and assorted medical paraphernalia. After consulting with Warwick, she took Sandrine's blood pressure, temperature, and injected her with a substance Warwick called an energizer.

Sandrine's headache cleared, and she left with Warwick. Silent empty, white corridors created an eerie atmosphere. One room they passed had a woman in bed, face covered with bandages, red hair flared on the pillow. Warwick told Sandrine this section of the building was a recovery spa for patients of famed plastic surgeon Dr. Perry Godfrey. He opened the door to a different suite showing Sandrine another patient bandaged from head to toe.

"She will be in twilight sleep during the most uncomfortable period of recovery."

Sandrine did not ask about her manuscript and notes. This was much bigger than a potential case of plagiarism. The pieces of a puzzle had begun to connect: Pyramid Prophecy, the Society of the Ten, and the quatrains. The final piece fit when Warwick brought her into an observation room with a one-way glass. A trace of cigar smoke lingered.

Sandrine saw Michele sleeping in a suite. *The greatest daughter taken* was in one of Madeleine's quatrains, and a mere pane of glass now separated her from Michele.

"Sandrine, the young Mademoiselle de Nostredame has been given a powerful growth serum. We cannot not wait for Michele to enter puberty naturally, for that might take another year or two. Your room will be on the other side of Michele's."

Because Warwick enjoyed gloating, Sandrine intended to extract every possible scrap of information from that egoist. They might have other ideas, but she meant to leave here alive and with Michele before *Le Crâne* arrived on his white charger according to Madeleine's quatrains.

Sandrine saw Michele's face become blissful. What dreams or visions could she be having?

***

Michele felt out of body walking on the pavement between massive pyramids, marble and stone buildings, surrounded by lush parks and tranquil lakes. The people on solid pathways seemed human but not like any she had seen before. They were tall, their skin sienna like the soil, in elegant garments of strange materials and design. No one noticed her. She must be invisible to them.

THE SORCERESS AND THE SKULL

The precise century and location of their civilization puzzled Michele. So did sculptures and bas-reliefs of bizarre animals flying and bounding among the population. Some resembled Goji. One hovered above as someone took her hand.

"My daughter. I have long awaited this providence to begin your education."

"You are Nostradamus."

"I am."

"How shall I address you?"

"Father."

Michele looked upward at the chimera. "Is that your pet?"

"No pet, he is your protector. He shall be with you forever. You may give him a name."

"I have. He is Goji."

Nostradamus led Michele inside a vast repository of manuscripts and tablets. "My daughter, here is the source and explanation of all the power, knowledge, and exceptional wisdom you shall have. More than ten thousand years older than the pyramids, that statue over there represents the man from whom we are descended. He preserved all this before a natural disaster occurred. Now you must go. Someone is coming for you. Fear nothing. They cannot harm you. We shall meet again."

CHAPTER 26
A THEORY OF TIME

Sunday morning there was a slight change of plans because Dante had no car. Doyle drove to Dr. Monash's home in St. Francis Woods and ranted. Last night, he found Sandrine's apartment ransacked. Then his father called at five in the morning warning him to forget the San Mateo estate because no judge down the Peninsula would issue a warrant for that address.

More salient, at seven this morning the Deputy Chief of Missing Persons again ordered Conlon to focus on his homicide cases because several of the more important guests at the gala filed complaints about his intrusion last night.

Doyle investigated further anyway. He learned the San Mateo estate was for sale, and the Society of the Ten leased it for the night. Worse, a friend in the Missing Persons Unit told him *they had no record* of Michele's disappearance.

"Marco, it is as if she never existed. Regardless, I contacted the ICPC, the International Criminal Police Commission, for information about Mrs. Desaix, Michele, and Sandrine. They promised a reply. Otherwise, I am on my own."

***

Dante brought the quatrains, his sketchpad, and Cadoux's reference book into Dr. Monash's Loos style home and introduced him to Conlon. Art Deco furniture filled the living room. Nineteenth and early twentieth century Symbolist and Art Nouveau paintings covered the walls. The psychiatrist's study had etchings by Dürer and Rembrandt hanging between bookcases. Manila folders and a recorder lay atop his desk.

When Dante complimented the art and furniture, Monash lamented he lived alone in too big a home for one person. His son was stationed with the Army of Occupation in Germany, and his married daughter and son-in-law resided in Seattle.

Monash offered them coffee and assorted danishes. Dante described what he knew about Michele's abduction and all Sandrine had told him about MacAndrew and the Society of the Ten. He gave Monash the quatrains with all his notes. The psychiatrist did not need to see Cadoux's book. He had his own copy.

Monash's excitement was palpable as he looked at the quatrains through clear protective plastic envelopes. "If these are not forgeries, you have a veritable treasure here. Each quatrain would be worth millions."

"That's why I cannot let anyone have them. They are my ward's property."

Monash consulted his copy of Cadoux's book and repeated the author's conclusion that the Seer's secretary, Jean Morel, penned all writings attributed to Nostradamus.

"Look here. The handwriting of your quatrains does not match this photo in the book of Morel's penmanship."

Monash asked if he could extract a piece of the paper to have its age verified. Dante consented, and with scissors and a tweezer, Monash removed a fragment from a corner and placed it in a sachet. He next scanned through each quatrain and separated them into two piles: those mentioning The Byzantine and *Verbedieu*, and the rest in which *the daughter*, *Le Crâne* and *La blond d'Hiver* appeared alone. Translating them would be difficult, but not impossible. Monash looked forward to the challenge of making an accurate interpretation.

"Marco, Inspector Conlon, do you believe a person can have the gift of precognition?"

"Given all that has happened this week, and my meeting with Lefton, I have to concede it is possible. Still, I find it difficult to believe that Nostradamus wrote specific quatrains about Sandrine and me four centuries ago."

"Inspector?"

"I am an agnostic regarding precognition."

"There is a Time Theory that may explain precognition. It was developed by an Irish aeronautical engineer, J. W. Dunne."

Dante and Conlon had not heard of the man or his theory.

***

After more coffee, Monash described the essence of Dunne's theory that all moments in time are taking place at once at the same time, and in the end, it explains *how*, not *why* anyone could have even the slightest glimpse of a future event. Yet, if this theory were indeed proven to be fact, it would convince the most demanding skeptic that a gifted seer like Nostradamus could see and predict true future events.

A physicist might explain it with complicated equations, as Einstein did with his Theory of Relativity. Monash preferred to use words and cite examples. He began with the three basic dimensions of space: length, width, and depth. Time was the Fourth Dimension, and according to Dunne's Time Theory, the Fifth and Sixth Dimensions of Time also existed. Thus, the theory posed three spatial and three dimensions of time, all inseparable.

Monash asked Dante and Conlon to imagine they were standing on top of a tall building where they saw a speeding car turn the corner. At the same instant, a child ran into the street. From their spatial position on the roof, they could predict what would happen below. If one could bridge traditional concepts of space and time, he would be able to perceive the future.

Monash suggested Dante and Conlon erase all concepts regarding Time in linear terms of past, present, and future, or, in other words, before, now, and after. Another concept of Time existed, a Great All-At-Once: whereas we experience the present, the evanescent *now* of the Great All-At-Once.

Monash drew a straight line on a sheet of paper to represent the Fourth Dimension, a before-now-after line in which one experienced events in succession.

"The Present exists. Past and Future do not. The Fourth Dimension is a series of brief, elusive *nows*, instantly here, instantly gone."

Monash drew more lines and explained how the Fifth Dimension of Time formed a limitless plane, a surface to the before-now-after line of the Fourth Dimension where all actual and possible *nows* of any given moment existed.

Monash explained further that the *potential* of each moment did not come and go, as each moment itself came and went. The Time Theory postulated that each potential *now* became eternal, imperishable.

"As typical products of Western Civilization, we have been conditioned to see the Fourth Dimensional line as having no beginning and no end. That is our concept of eternity. However, it is the Fifth Dimension of Time, which is true eternity according to the Theory. There, in simultaneous existence are all the before-now-after lines of successive Time. Limitless in number. Extending infinitely. In the Sixth Dimension, all possible *nows* are actualized."

"Are you telling us each act or move we do *not* make but *might* have made, the opportunities we missed the poetic road not taken but might have, all are actualized in the Sixth Dimension?"

"Each one of them, Marco."

"Parallel universes?"

"You might say that, which is why, if this Time Theory holds, it would explain the greatest paradox associated with precognition."

"Which is?"

"As an example, you dream you are on a plane flying to New York. It crashes. You awaken and realize it is the same flight you are supposed to take today. You cancel your flight. Later you learn the plane crashed. Now the paradox. If you saw your future and changed it, then the future cannot exist. If your future exists, then you cannot change it."

Monash suggested that if one visualized "the" future, it was *one* future among the infinite possibilities of the Fifth Dimension being actualized in the Sixth Dimension.

That led Dante to speculate about his past and future. If his fiancée had accepted his damaged face and wed him, how might his life be different from what it was now? What future actions might lead him to a woman who would? Conlon wondered the same about his choices and lack of a mate.

***

After another break, Monash began to explain how the future might be foreseen with accuracy through the other half of the Time Theory.

"Within each of us exist three Observers, for want of a better word. Observer-One is our conscious and deals with our perceived real world. Observer-Two is our subconscious, which is liberated when we sleep or go into a trance. It ranges over the Fourth, Fifth, and Sixth dimensions of Time and reports what it sees and experiences back to Observer-One, our conscious. We call those messages dreams, visions, and prophecies. But Observer-Two, our subconscious, has no experiences with the real world of our consciousness. It cannot differentiate between important and unimportant, the possible and the absurd, past, present or future. Observer-Two reports what it has seen during the hours a person is asleep or in a trance so when we are awake, our memory of the report is confused and jumbled."

Dante believed he had a rough understanding of the Time Theory except for one omission. "What about Observer-Three?"

"That is what we call the eternal soul, but it need not concern you at this time."

"What do you think, Doyle?'

"It may be possible Nostradamus had a clear picture of what the Seer's Observer-Two reported after his dreams and trances."

"If the Time Theory is valid." Monash held a quatrain

from the stack at his right. "Now, let us see if there is anything here that will help us locate Michele."

Dante looked at Monash's drawing of the three dimensions of time. "I can see where one could get all caught up in this Time Theory business."

"Young man, let me share with you the wisdom I received from a great teacher of science and life. Do not ever dwell on the Time Theory."

"Did he say why?"

"Yes, he did. That way lies madness."

CHAPTER 27
SOLILOQUY OF A TRUE BELIEVER

Sunday morning in the observation room, Warwick told Sandrine it was time for her to know The Society of the Ten's sacred mission. He looked upward and praised the Lord for delivering Michele to the Society.

"I believe in an infinite God, the Son and Savior Jesus Christ, and Their divinely inspired words in the Bible. Nostradamus possessed the original sources of wisdom taken from the Great Pyramid by his tribe of Issachar during the Exodus. The Scriptural prophets used those same sources. Therefore, Nostradamus wrote the quatrains under Divine guidance."

"Did he really?"

Warwick did not hear Sandrine's ironic tone. The Society of the Ten's well connected membership through its enormous wealth and influence elects Congressmen and Parliamentarians, appoints men to the highest military rank. We place our people in control of natural resources and key industries in the United States, Great Britain, Northern

Europe, the white Commonwealth nations, and Japan.

"What has all that to do with Michele?"

"She has a role to play in our Society's grand scheme to fulfill its destiny through a surprise-free future and avoid unforeseen, unplanned-for events, which make theoretical projections worthless, such as accidents, illnesses, earthquakes, hurricanes, and other natural disasters."

Sandrine thought Warwick exceeded his reputation as a boring drone whose attempts at humor always fell flat among his students.

"Learning the future is no spectator sport."

Sandrine did not smile at Warwick's feeble jest.

"Our Society must control its course toward the future with the power and the freedom to usher in a new age, a world of peace for True Israel, and a racially pure world. First we need to know the immediate future in detail and learn how best to discover the identity of and to prevail over the Third Antichrist. The crucial years lay ahead between 1999 and 2020. The final battle will take place in the lands of the original Ten Tribes, Biblical Israel."

Warwick raised his voice as if addressing a congregation. He quoted New Testament passages relating to Armageddon and the Beast of the Apocalypse, followed by Nostradamus' mention of the Three Antichrists. "In all books about Nostradamus I have read, the authors write that Napoleon was the first Antichrist, Hitler the second, and godless communism the third. Amateurs and fools wrote those interpretations. .History and recent events have proven them wrong."

Sandrine asked the question Warwick expected to hear. "Then who are the Antichrists in your opinion?"

"The godless totalitarianism of Fascism, Nazism, and state socialism under the guise of communism, *that* is the

First Antichrist. The worship of false material gods of money and power, sexual obsession and perversions, race mixing and moral degeneration are the Second Antichrist."

"And the Third Antichrist?"

"The numbers did not lie. The Beast of the Apocalypse, as described in the New Testament, is known by its mark of 666. Three sixes equal eighteen. Eight plus one equals nine. The Society suspects who or what the Third Antichrist might be, but first we must interpret the quatrains that identify the Beast. And Michele, asleep on the other side of that his glass, will soon reveal where those prophecies that identify the Beast have been secreted."

Warwick rambled and repeated much of Mrs. Lambert's lecture on Pyramid prophecy, and his eyes continued to fascinate Sandrine. They had been unfocused from the start as if he did not see her.

Warwick abruptly ended his harangue and made eye contact with Sandrine.

"Come with me. Many questions you have not yet asked shall be answered."

CHAPTER 28
IN TUSCAN LANDS?

Sunday noon Monash held one of the quatrains and gave a caveat that other translators might come to different conclusions. According to his interpretation, Michele had been taken to the land of the Etruscans, Tuscany in northern Italy, or Anatolia in Turkey.

He showed Dante and Conlon his translation, which was identical to Michele's:

> Be gone, flee from Etruscan soil,
> Walls, edifices, the bottom raised to the top;
> The prized child, captive of The Byzantine,
> Faith too great, through play life lost.

The quatrain described a severe earthquake "... the bottom raised to the top." Monash had selected it for another reason: Etruscan soil or land was *Terre Etrusque* in the original French. Monash had put aside other verses containing *Etrusque.*

Dante and Conlon read Monash's translation and interpretation of the next quatrain. Michele had been abducted by someone called *Verbedieu,* likely to be The Byzantine, and taken to Etruscan soil, that would place her in northern Italy, where the Etruscans flourished before the Romans conquered them, or in Turkey. By playing Nostradamus' game, one could extract *Turque* from *Etrusque.* Many historians accepted as fact that the Etruscans migrated from Anatolia to the Italian peninsula.

Monash conceded that whether or not Nostradamus made a few accurate guesses against overwhelming odds, he was a genius encryptor. "There is something else I find interesting and perplexing. Here, and in several other quatrains, The Byzantine is called *Verbedieu,* Word of God from the French."

Monash translated as Dante and Conlon read together:

Tard le Byzantin, Verbedieu, se viendra repentir,
De n'avior mis a mort son adversaire;
Mais viendra bien a plus haut consentir,
Que tout, son sang, part mort deffaire.

Byzantine, Word of God, shall come to repent too late,
Of not putting his adversary to death;
But he shall consent to do a greater thing,
Which is to cause all of his blood to be put to death.

Dante failed so far to come up with a decent anagram for Verbedieu. Then his personal light bulb lit. Word of God could be translated into other languages favored by Nostradamus. The Byzantines spoke Greek, and *Verbedieu,*

Word of God, could be *Logos* or even *Theologos*. That much Greek he remembered from his classes at Lowell.

He told Conlon and Monash that was a name he had not thought of in years. Constantine Theologos was one of those Merchants of Death blamed for causing World War I so they might profit from selling weapons and munitions to both sides.

Conlon's face reddened. Veins on his face and neck appeared ready to burst. "Theologos. That genocidal slime."

"Doyle, what the hell's the matter with you?"

Conlon, remembered history better than Dante remembered Greek for personal reasons. Theologos had been into more than munitions. He had been residing in the Ottoman Empire at the end of the nineteenth century and during the First World War. He helped organize the Armenian massacres in 1894-95 and a greater atrocity during WWI.

"Marco, Dr. Monash, it was not out of religious, national, or ethnic hatred. Theologos worked with the Turks to slaughter my mother's people, butcher most of my maternal family, millions of Armenians, all for profit."

Monash's soothing voice calmed Conlon. "Inspector, all you say is true, but it would be impossible for Constantine Theologos to be the *Verbedieu* of these quatrains. If he were alive today, he would be, let me calculate, yes, he would be no less than one-hundred-and-five years old."

He pushed the quatrains across his desk toward Dante and said, "I have done my best."

Dante thanked Monash and placed the quatrains in the oversized envelope. The psychiatrist's translations had brought him no closer to finding Michele. Furthermore, Monash's hypothesis did not answer one important question: If the land of The Byzantine was either Italy or Turkey, why was there so much activity here in the City?

Lefton had said Michele was somewhere near his home. Dante trusted the psychic's gifts more than the psychiatrist's analysis.

"Before you leave, Marco, tell me why you brought your sketchpad."

Dante showed Monash and Conlon one sketch of Michele on a hospital bed and another of the physician in attendance.

Monash gasped, horrified. He identified the man in the sketch as Dr. Hartmann Lusser, once regarded as the world's foremost developer of hormones for rejuvenation, growth for stunted children, and acceleration of the onset of puberty for late maturers. Lusser had worked with Josef Mengele at Auschwitz experimenting on live children to perfect his serum. Like his colleague, he was high on the list of wanted war criminals.

Michele had been captive for three days. All that time, Lusser must have been injecting the girl with his serum to accelerate her puberty. If it had not been perfected, Michele would be in great peril.

***

Sunday noon Warwick brought Sandrine through a pair of security doors into a spacious windowless room. Three men and one woman isolated in cubicle, read and wrote at tables like medieval scribes. Each wore pale blue pajamas beneath white laboratory coats with coded nametags. Warwick identified them as experts and pedant masters of Greek, Latin, Hebrew, anagrams, ciphers, astrology, and tricks of occult obscurantists. They had been interpreting each word penned by Nostradamus in every possible way to be compared with Professor Cadoux's translations at a central location.

Warwick emphasized they preferred to recruit volunteers, individuals of great ability with unquestioning faith in their particular areas of expertise. The experts worked under a self-demanding schedule. Nurses gave energizing injections and liquid refreshment to scholars who showed signs of fatigue.

"We regret the average true believer lasts about one month. The cause? Impossible to verify. The consensus believes Nostradamus created the quatrains in such a way that those who delve deeply into them short-circuit their synapses, meaning the experts become brain dead. After burnout is confirmed, we euthanize them. Their most useful organs are harvested, refrigerated and sent to other facilities scattered throughout the world for life-extending experiments and transplants. A helicopter carries the unusable remains to a crematorium."

Does he ever take a breath?

"A commotion at one of the cubicles caught Warwick's attention. "Look, Sandrine, over there. That is what I mean by burnout."

They went to a young man who had collapsed at his desk. Warwick spun him around, and Sandrine studied with detached interest her first encounter with the vacant stare of a burned out scholar. Warwick shrugged as if it were a common occurrence and ordered attendants to carry him away.

"Who is he?"

"Peter Poons from Amsterdam, a gifted and intuitive astrologer, one of the best two or three in the world. It will be difficult to replace him." Warwick grinned at Sandrine. "We have been more fortunate in the area of Old and Medieval

French."

He brought Sandrine upstairs again to her bedroom suite next to Michele's room. A stack of Nostradamus' prophecies, a ream of paper, and a smaller pile of fourteen quatrains she recognized lay atop a desk. Someone had taken them from her apartment.

Warwick showed Sandrine a large box filled with shredded paper. "Your manuscript and notes were of no use to us. We shall learn later how you acquired these unpublished quatrains that mention *La Blond d'Hiver*. First, you will translate and interpret them for us. Next, you will verify Cadoux's interpretations of the entire published works of Nostradamus. We will bring you to Michele after she awakens. Notify me the moment she shows even the slightest sign of precognition."

Alone in her suite, Sandrine exhaled to relieve tension. She had needed much self-control not to interrupt and speak her mind during Warwick's bloviating. The Byzantine would not be pleased he revealed so much.

Warwick disgusted Sandrine. She understood one unintended revelation. That the lightweight showed her the Scriptorium and spoke of the burnouts meant he intended for her to die here.

Sandrine suppressed a temptation to smile. Warwick, that pompous twit, had no idea he had delivered Michele to her. Sooner than anticipated, she would take control of the girl.

CHAPTER 29
IMPATIENT VISITOR

Dante returned home early Sunday afternoon. Mié and Goji awaited him in his studio. Why had the chimera disappeared the other day, and where had it gone?

He changed clothes and painted a new portrait of Sandrine until before seven when the doorbell rang. Serafino brushed past him and hurried into the den. He went behind the wet bar and poured a double shot of hundred proof I. W. Harper bourbon in a snifter.

"*Maledizione*, Marco, what's going on? I haven't seen or heard from you since Tuesday. Have you gotten any painting done?"

"I do have some oils to show you."

Dante went to a dark recessed corner of his den and showed Serafino one of his completed portraits of Sandrine. "What do you think?"

Serafino took the canvas from Dante. "Marco, this is great. No bull. A masterpiece. It's still wet."

"I completed it an hour ago."

153

THE SORCERESS AND THE SKULL

"You got any more?"

"Don't get paranoid, Al. Wait here a moment." Dante went into the kitchen, where he put the other portraits after Serafino called to alert him he was coming.

When Dante returned with the canvases, Serafino scrutinized each one. "Beautiful. Exquisite. Don't let your models get away." Serafino held another of the oils to catch the full impact of the artificial light in the den. "Like I said before, these are so good it hurts. But I refuse to get an ulcer worrying if you can deliver enough paintings and graphics for your exhibit." He poured another double shot of the I.W. "Marco, tomorrow I want to see you at the gallery with these canvases. We have to begin making graphics."

"I'd planned to."

"Good." Serafino selected one of Sandrine's portraits and another of Michele. "Mazurek came up with a great idea for setting the best three in an elaborate cabinet so that when it's opened they resemble a Renaissance ... damn, what's the fancy word he used?"

"Triptych?"

"Yeah, that's the word."

"I like that concept."

"I'll get Mazurek working on it. I may have some other interesting subjects for you to paint as well. Now tell me, where's the kid, your ward? Something fishy is going on around you. My crew heard rumors about a serial slasher operating in this neighborhood and that two victims died near your house. .Nothing has been reported on radio or in the newspapers."

Dante knew better than to hold back anything from Serafino. He told Al all that happened after he and Michele left the studio Tuesday afternoon to his meetings with Lefton and Monash. Dante showed Serafino the unpublished

154

quatrains.

"What the hell. You know I can't read French."

"Neither can I, but they mentioned me as the Skull, Sandrine as the Winter Blonde, and describe Michele's descent from Nostradamus."

An hour later, Serafino had consumed half the I.W. bottle without showing any effects. "So let me get this straight. The two men killed in front of your home Tuesday night were involved in a failed attempt to kidnap Michele."

"Yes."

"But you can't say who offed them. Then she was kidnaped on Thursday in broad daylight at her high school, and the Winter Blond of your portraits disappeared Saturday night at some hoity-toity function." Serafino pointed at the bar. "Odd, damn odd, Marco."

"What is?"

"That gargoyle next to the bottle of Harper on the bar counter. I didn't notice it there before."

Neither had Dante. He didn't know how best to explain Goji to Serafino and instead reminded him it was in Michele's *Little Sorceress* portrait.

"Marco, are the cops making her abduction a priority?"

"Strange, but they are not. Conlon is being pressured to forget about searching for Michele, and Missing Persons has put her case on the back burner."

"Not to worry, Marco. I've got several boys in blue on my payroll. They'll tell me what's going on. I promise you, my crew will be working the grapevine, and I'll let you know report what they hear. I want Michele found soon so you can concentrate on painting full time."

CHAPTER 30
FANATICS

On Monday, Sandrine had not slept or eaten much since Saturday morning, even though she was entitled, if that was the proper word. She worked eighteen hours shifts, with a four-hour break for nourishment and rest. She finished obfuscating for her own purposes the true meanings of the fourteen unpublished quatrains the Society had stolen from her apartment.

Next, Sandrine took on the monumental task of confirming or offering alternate interpretations for Cadoux's translations of Nostradamus' published quatrains, sixains, epistles, and letters. Isolated in her suite, she had not spoken to any of the other experts. Like the true believers, she became involved in her work as if nothing else mattered.

***

Through a peephole, The Woman watched Sandrine writing at her desk. Anger altered her lacquered features.

156

"Warwick, have you lost your mind? I do not want Dr. Arnoul to be another burnout. I need her. She is the best in the world. She is the unique one who can understand everything Michele says. I cannot afford to lose either. And you, Warwick, I order you to leave Sandrine alone. Go now."

The Woman turned her back to Warwick and went to Michele's suite where Dr. Lusser attended the sleeping girl. "Is the serum working yet?"

The Endocrinologist could not say for certain. "We shall know more after she awakens, but the signs are promising. I still believe it will take a week or two at most for the serum to work."

Lusser suggested The Woman move closer to Michele and listen to her mumbling, not in French, but in a language neither understood.

She stood over Michele. Was the girl dreaming or seeing the future? Sandrine could not be readied soon enough. This living child was worth more than all the scribblings of Nostradamus heaped together, and if forced to choose between them, The Woman would ignite all the manuscripts herself. Michele as a living prophet would see all future possibilities The Woman needed to know.

She saw Warwick had followed. "What?" The Woman snarled, "You are still here? Do you not know how to obey orders? I have held my tongue until now. I am furious with you. Fool. Idiot. You presumed to take Sandrine on a tour of the clinic. You babbled incessantly to impress her. You told her what she should never have known. Most stupid of all, you went out of your way to let her see a burnout. Warwick, your inflated ego may be the death of you. Now, get out. Get out of my sight."

***

THE SORCERESS AND THE SKULL

Sandrine awakened from a deep sleep, refreshed and eager to work. She resented being led from her desk to a spa. Sandrine suffered through a thorough bath and an herbal rubdown combined with aromatherapy on a massage table. Servants treated, washed, and coiffed her hair into a chignon following with a manicure and a pedicure.

After the grooming, Sandrine put on a fresh pair of pajamas and slippers. Taken back to her room, she was startled and not at all pleased the desk and papers were missing.

Warwick entered behind attendants pushing two large carts; one with a warm wilted spinach salad, escargot, and a thick filet mignon; and the other with a superb white Montrachet in an ice bucket and a powerful Richebourg. Warwick poured the red Burgundy into a crystal decanter. He advised her to eat and drink well and left.

Sandrine ate voraciously and tried to ascertain why she was given the so-called royal treatment. Her curiosity intensified during crème brulé and double espresso, and peaked when Warwick and MacAndrew entered with a bottle of XO cognac and three glasses. The latter wore a burgundy uniform with patches of Israelite tribes on his sleeves and silver eagles on his shoulder straps. Warwick informed Sandrine that MacAndrew was Chief of Security among other tasks. He poured and passed a glass to Sandrine. "You're looking much better now."

Sandrine suspected Warwick's superior must have given him a dressing down to end his arrogance toward her, but his natural inclination to be self-important had returned.

MacAndrew saluted Sandrine with his glass and told her they had decided it was best she move into Michele's suite. That was why her desk and the quatrains were in the girl's sitting room. MacAndrew ordered Sandrine to record anything Michele might say while asleep. "Befriend her."

Sandrine stifled an urge to laugh until Warwick and MacAndrew left. Befriend Michele? Of course she would. Those arrogant *cochons* thought they were in charge; instead, they had given her the greatest prize of all,

***

Monday morning, Mazurek arrived with a van for Dante, who brought all his completed oils to the gallery except the wet portrait of Sandrine. After Serafino and Mazurek discussed the framing and creating serigraphs with Dante, he drove a loaner car to Union Street near his home. Dante found a Thompson street guide for the City, but none for the adjacent Bay Area communities. He lunched at *Bella Venezia*, left a message for Conlon to find the guides he wanted, and went home.

By late afternoon, Dante decided failure had become his doppelganger. The Thompson San Francisco guide was useless. Michele had been gone for a week, Sandrine since Saturday. He could not think of any way to locate them other than through a psychic connection with Michele, or Tuscan street names in the Thompson guide.

Mié shrieked below the table where Dante left Sandrine's portrait to dry and ran from the studio. The horizontal 96" x 64" canvas was his largest to date. Last night, he had painted Sandrine all in white except for her green eyes, with arms extended above a pair of Snowy Owls, wings spread and talons extended. All three hovered above a sere surreal landscape as if they were predators hunting for prey. The Winter Blonde's hair flowed behind her in the wind.

Now the oils moved on their own except for the original

colors, Dante's name, the date and title, but to his astonishment Sandrine's hair spread Medusa-like in all directions, eyes suggesting madness. Malevolence infused the studio when the Winter Blonde hovered over Michele lying on a bed unconscious. Dante blinked. That same instant, the painting returned to its original state. He stared at every square inch of the canvas to be sure.

Back to normal but still shaken, Dante left the studio and went to the den. He poured a scotch on the rocks and settled in his armchair.

The doorbell rang.

***

Dante opened the front door expecting Conlon. Instead, four teenage boys wearing Lowell athletic sweaters stood outside on the steps. The tallest introduced his teammates, "... and I'm Blake Townsend, Mr. Dante. We are Michele's classmates, and we're worried about her."

He led the boys into the den. They gathered at a group of photos hanging on one wall, some showing Dante in his Lowell and Cal football uniforms, and others with his teammates. Medals and certificates for valor hung near them. The boys had not expected him to be an alumnus of their high school and asked how successful his teams had been.

Dante put them more at ease by offering soft drinks from the wet bar. "I appreciate it that you are so concerned for Michele."

The boys conferred. Townsend spoke for them. "We all like Michele. She has been tutoring us in different subjects."

Townsend's revelation piqued Dante's curiosity. Michele never mentioned she had been tutoring anyone.

"I want Michele found for another reason, sir. I like her a lot. I asked her to be my date for the Junior Prom. Michele said she'd speak to you about it last Thursday."

Townsend was clean cut, good looking, about six-two, lean and sinewy, well mannered too. Dante tried to imagine the boy and tiny Michele dancing together. No point in upsetting Townsend by telling him he would not allow her to go to the prom or even a movie. Michele was too young to date anyone. He had not considered another responsibility that came with being Michele's guardian, protecting her from boys like he had been.

"Mr. Dante, sir? We want to help you find Michele."

"I thank you for the offer, but we are dealing with very unpleasant individuals. I am sure your parents would disapprove of your becoming involved."

"We don't care. Please, tell us what we can do."

"Sit tight and wait. Let the professionals deal with it. I am convinced that Michele will be brought home soon."

Dante wished he were as confident as he made himself sound.

After the boys left, Dante returned to his studio and set a blank canvas on the easel in the hope Michele would contact him. She did not. He drew Michele full face and profiles. He wanted another psychic connection. It did not come. Mié and Goji stared at Dante from the couch.

"Okay, Mié, will you please do your cat thing? And Goji, whatever it is you are supposed to do, do it. Help me find Michele. At least do something more than collect dust."

***

Monday night, rested and refreshed, Sandrine sat beside Michele with a magnetic tape recorder MacAndrew provided.

161

Her desk had been set against a wall in the girl's spacious suite.

Michele awakened and appeared to be alert although her eyes were unfocused. MacAndrew stood on the other side of the bed. "Arnoul, speak to her and begin your translation."

When Sandrine attempted to hold Michele's hand, the girl tensed and pulled it away.

"Michele, I am Sandrine. *Je suis* Sandrine. I am Marco's friend. Remember me? I am here to help you. Do not be afraid."

"Sandrine."

"Yes."

"*La Blond d'Hiver. La blonde dame.*"

"Tell her to speak louder."

Michele moved farther away from Sandrine. "*L'hain ... discorde ... conflit ... ennemi.*"

"Arnoul, what is the girl saying?"

Sandrine translated the words for MacAndrew, but not their context. "Hatred, discord, conflict, an enemy. So far, it is all too vague and disconnected. I will have to transcribe everything so I can make sense of them."

Sandrine whispered in Old French so MacAndrew would not be able to hear words he did understand. "Michele, tell Goji where you are. Tell him, and he will reveal our location to Marco."

Michele sat on the edge of her bed and whispered to Sandrine, "You are no less my enemy than The Byzantine." She closed her eyes and telepathed, *Goji, Mié, help me. Speak to Marco.*

MacAndrew moved to Sandrine's side of the bed and slapped her shoulder. "Dammit, what's going on?"

Sandrine resisted an urge to demonstrate on MacAndrew why she earned a black belt in karate and kept an even tone.

"I am encouraging Michele to speak more coherently. Your presence is unnerving her. It will be better if you leave us alone."

"All right, Arnoul, but be assured we shall be watching and listening in the observation room."

Alone with Michele, Sandrine gripped her shoulders and continued whispering in Old French. "Listen to me. I know you may have divined who I am, what I am. You cannot change your future. That I am part of it, part of it forever. The same as Marco. So your Aunt Madeleine's quatrains have stated. Deny it all you want, but I shall always be part of your life. Do you understand?"

Michele stared horrified at Sandrine as the blonde's coiffed hair unraveled. "Leave me alone."

"I shall never leave you alone. Never, not ever.

CHAPTER 31
SERENDIPITY

Tuesday had been a day and night of no progress and much driving around the City. Wednesday morning Dante managed to find current Thompson Guides for the North and East Bay communities but none for the Peninsula. Conlon did not leave any message at *Bella Venezia*, and a search for Tuscan street names in the North and East Bay guides so far had produced nothing. One piece of good news: at least Dante's car had been repaired, and Serafino sent one of his men to collect the loaner.

About midnight, he fell asleep until Mié awakened him at five in the morning. Groggy, he fed the cat and brewed a pot of strong coffee.

Conlon arrived an hour later. With a Thompson Peninsula guide for Dante. He cursed and explained why he could not help Dante search for Michele.

"The Department continues to deny my requests for progress reports from Missing Persons. Every clerk and lower ranking officer said they were inundated with multiple assignments from this Captain, that Commander, and the Chief when I asked for their help, even those with whom I have the best working relationships, including my own father.

Conlon paused and glanced at the quatrains Dante left on the sofa "Still trying to figure them out?"

"So far it's an exercise in futility. I cannot make any translations because I do not know French. My instincts tell me Michele will contact me one way or another, on canvas or some other way."

Mié shrieked. The cat leaped from the desk, pushing the guides and Goji to the floor, and flew into Dante's arms. He set Mié on the desk and stroked her, but she would not stop meowing. Dante saw Goji perched on his *Thompson Peninsula Guide*. The guide had fallen open to a page containing a map of the hills south of Los Gatos. He lifted Goji to the desk beside Mié, which calmed her, and he picked up the guide. Unbelievable, impossible, yet the page showed a side road named Milano Drive. In the hills south of Los Gatos. The quatrains had given him the necessary clues after all.

"Look at this, Doyle."

"I'd be surprised if there were no more surprises."

Dante drew a circle on the map. "This is our *Terre Etrusque*. Milano Drive. And Tuscany's capital city is Milano, Milan."

"You're telling me Nostradamus knew what street would be in Los Gatos four centuries later?"

"I have to work with what I've got." Dante scratched the underside of Mié's chin and patted Goji's head. "Thanks, guys."

Mié rewarded Dante with high-rev purring, and Goji's eyes reflected stronger light.

Conlon studied the map. "Milano drive seems to go nowhere. No side streets to indicate any homes, but wait a minute. I remember now. There used to be a Benedictine monastery in those hills, years before the war. They made a great brandy and decent wine. Then it was abandoned. To cover all that property, I'll need more than a search warrant. We'll require plenty of backup too. Forget warrants, and we can't go in through the front door."

"Then we'll try the back, Doyle. We need to reconnoiter every terrain feature in the area. FInd out everything you can about that monastery and its current owner. Can you at least get me that?"

"I know where they'd be registered. I'll handle it, Marco, but I won't be able to get us any men from the Department."

"I'm sure Serafino and Rafe Mazurek will join us. And Al might bring his crew."

"Mazurek? I'll never forget him. He played for St. Mary's and was the dirtiest lineman of them all. Mazurek is the s.o.b who injured my knee and kept me from qualifying for the Draft. How does he fit in?"

"Rafe is Serafino's framer, mine too, and he'll be worth a squad if the going gets rough. We'll make our plans during the day, move tomorrow night and count on surprise and luck."

"I have to report at headquarters. In between, I'll find out what I can about Theologos."

"I will have to figure out things my own way."

CHAPTER 32
CONSTANTINE THEOLOGOS

Thursday morning, but day of the week, hour of the day, they mattered not to Sandrine. Time became meaningless in Michele's suite. To make matters worse, Sandrine's breasts ached, a sure sign her period was due within the next forty-eight hours. Head heavy and body weak, she resisted sleep.

Sandrine listened to the latest taping and typed every word Michele had spoken. She translated, juxtaposed lines, and rearranged letters of potential anagrams. Her temples throbbed. Massaging them did no good, and she fainted at the desk.

Sandrine awakened on a gray leather couch in a research library. Warwick and MacAndrew stood over her. When Sandrine attempted to move her limbs, Warwick reached out with a cup of steaming brew. "Here, it is an energizing concentrate developed by Dr. Lusser."

Sandrine drank the concoction and frowned at its unfamiliar, cloying taste. Warwick sat beside her.

"Things are moving faster than anyone anticipated. The

serum has worked, as you must know. Michele's mind has matured ahead of her body development. Lusser has promised us Michele's maiden period will arrive within the next two weeks. Everything the girl has said to you confirms she has Nostradamus' gifts, and more. Michele will lead us to where the unpublished prophecies have been secreted."

"And we'll use the girl to see a future that even Nostradamus did not have time to write down," MacAndrew added.

The intercom buzzed. Warwick listened and beckoned MacAndrew to leave the room with him. Now alone, Sandrine felt the full effect of the energizer. More than wide-awake, she became hyperactive with an uncontrollable need to move about.

Sandrine stopped pacing the floor when she read CONSTANTINE THEOLOGOS emblazoned in gold on the covers of three black scrapbooks lying on a nearby table.

Theologos, Verbedieu. Word of God.

Sandrine sat on a couch by the table and opened the first volume to a Karsh photograph of an elegant, olive complexioned man. A trimmed mustache and white beard suggested a nineteenth-century European monarch. At first glance, Sandrine thought he looked avuncular. Then she stared into the man's deep-set eyes, merciless eyes, and imagined his mustache and beard hid cruel hard lines around the mouth.

Perhaps Theologos was the person giving Warwick and MacAndrew orders; but according to the gold embossed years of birth and death under his photo, he was born in 1830 at Izmir-Smyrna and died in 1935 at age 105.

Sandrine looked at more pages filled with photographs of Theologos and speed-read through the scrapbooks. Documents, letters, and messages set between media articles and photographs revealed that for material gain and self-aggrandizement Theologos had encouraged, financed, or caused most wars throughout the world between 1854 and World War II. With his American agents, he manipulated the great Stock Market Crash of 1929. In Germany, Theologos financed and facilitated Hitler's rise to power.

Sandrine heard a commotion outside the library. A woman entered accompanied by Warwick and MacAndrew. She wore a royal purple and gold robe over a matching silk lounging suit. Tinted red hair crowned a pale, lacquer-smooth face identical to the Comparative Literature Department secretary at Cal, Miss Hale.

The Woman beckoned Sandrine to rise and come closer. Cold, remorseless porcelain blue eyes between brows and cheekbones seemed to have no connection to her face, as if a malignant alien beast lived in the shell of a human being.

***

The Woman sat in a gray leather armchair in the library alcove. MacAndrew and Warwick attended her, ready to obey any command without hesitation.

"You cannot be Miss Hale."

"You are correct. I had a plastic surgeon create several facial doubles for me to use when necessary."

"I had not expected *Verbedieu* to be a woman. You must be The Byzantine of the quatrains and a descendant of Constantine Theologos."

"My mother married the youngest son of the great Constantine Theologos. I was christened Irene Theologos. My mother, Moira Moray, was a direct descendant of the Stuarts and the House of David through Téa Tephi, daughter of Zedikiah, the last King of Israel."

MacAndrew's genealogical chart at the bookstore.

"Theologos does have a familiar ring to it, very much like some dynasty from The Byzantine Empire. The last one was Palaeologus, though, was it not?"

"And my antecedents. I see you have been reading about my grandfather. Constantine Theologos was an exceptional man. He began what I am about to complete. History offers many examples of great men leaving solid foundations for their still greater heirs to build upon. In England, Henry VII and Henry VIII created the England that made Elizabeth I great. In France, Louis XIV would have been nothing without Henry IV, Sully, and Cardinals Richelieu and Mazarin."

"All that is interesting, but what does it have to do with Nostradamus?"

"Everything, and no one can stop me."

"Stop you from doing what?"

"I am more supreme than any conqueror who ever lived, thanks to my vast inherited and accumulated wealth I control much of the world's sources of energy, food, and governments through surrogates, my. useful idiots. All that is not enough. I must possess omniscience to guarantee myself a surprise-free future. "To accomplish that, I must learn all Nostradamus saw, what Michele may yet see ...."

Warwick could not stay silent. "And we shall ensure Good triumphs over Evil. Israel, not those mongrelized Armenoid-Khazars. True Israel must prepare the way for the Second Coming of Our Lord. Then shall our Society of the Ten gather all pure-blooded Israelites tribe by tribe for the Great Day of Judgment."

"Warwick, this is not the time for one of your bombasts. Sandrine, I had you brought here to corroborate Pierre Cadoux's translations and verify their accuracy. You have been described as my adversary according to the prophecies of Nostradamus. Therefore, I believe it prudent to keep you near me until I am convinced I shall have no further use for your polymathic abilities." Irene gestured at the men. "Warwick, MacAndrew. Leave us. I wish to speak with Sandrine alone."

They did not protest, but Sandrine saw anger in their eyes.

***

Sandrine walked with Irene Theologos into a garden and topiary between the monastery and a clearing behind a hexagon-shaped building. When they sat beside each other on a stone bench, Irene took out a gold case from her robe. She removed two cigars, clipped their ends, and offered one to Sandrine, which she lit for her.

"Feel free to call me Irene. I thought it best to speak where we cannot be heard. My grandfather, Constantine Theologos believed Nostradamus wrote an accurate history of the entire future of mankind. Once my grandfather became aware of the unpublished prophecies, he determined to have them at all costs. He ordered his agents to find the de Nostredames, liquidate them, and take whatever prophecies they had. My grandfather was flattered his name and description often appeared in Nostradamus' prophecies, as you should be, *La Blond d'Hiver*."

Sandrine thought it significant Irene did not mention how she became the heir to Thologos' empire.

Irene resumed her narrative. In the summer of 1940 during the early days of the German occupation of Paris, she used the Nazis to help her search for surviving de Nostredames. An informer brought to her attention the name of a female prisoner arrested by the Gestapo who came from a family using a pathetic alias for de Nostredame. Irene, through her connection to the Nazis, received permission to interrogate Catherine Dastiel. Under drugs and through other methods of persuasion, she confirmed the prisoner was a direct descendant of Nostradamus, brilliant of mind but without any of the Seer's gifts. After more severe torture, Catherine Dastiel spoke of thousands of unpublished prophecies possessed by her family. She later escaped.

"From that time, I have committed my vast resources to seek and obtain those prophecies, with or without the cooperation of the de Nostredames."

"So you can ensure that The Society of the Ten triumphs over the Third Antichrist?"

"Do not take me for a fool. Do you really think I believe any of their ridiculous assertions?"

"Then you are not a true believer?"

"I believe in myself. No one else, nothing else. The Society of the Ten is merely one of several necessary tools to ensure I achieve my goal. As for the Antichrists, there could be dozens of possibilities regarding who might be the third. By now, your research should have revealed how Nostradamus used that name as a metaphor for any tyrant. He had to seem religious for fear of the Inquisition. Those Jew-converts often took on the most pious of names when they insincerely embraced the so-called True Faith. De Nostredame. Of Our Lady. How presumptuous."

"If you have no religious motivations, what do you plan to do after you achieve both omniscience and omnipotence?"

"Rule the world and rid it of religious fanatics like Warwick and MacAndrew, liquidate other worthless scum, and end the over-breeding of inferior sub-humans."

"And when you die? Then what? You have no heirs to inherit your power and knowledge. Who will carry on with your plans?"

"Die? I believe the secret to a longer healthy life lies in learning the future. There will be medical discoveries and techniques that can prolong life, perhaps even prevent death."

"And if you do not discover all that in time before you die?"

"Some with great wealth create charitable foundations. Others seek power. A few support extreme politicians for malicious sport. I shall have had a very good run of successes and a good read of the future, so that if I must die, my curiosity will have been fulfilled. But, before then, I shall have drained from Michele every last dollop of knowledge she possesses. Perhaps even mold her in my image to succeed me if I can trust her. Yes, I would make her my sole heir. Before that, I shall have dealt with *Le Crâne*, as I shall with you, unless ..."

"Unless what?"

Irene scanned the topiary to verify no one was near. "I had considered disposing of you today, but now I prefer to make you a proposition, Sandrine. If you are wise, you will accept my offer, and given what I have learned about you, I believe you will find it most attractive. I trust my instincts, and I sense your goals diverge from those of *Le Crâne*. You may be the one person in the world who can translate everything Michele says. I offer you a position as her constant companion."

"For how long?"

"As long as she lives. You will have everything money can buy."

"Except personal freedom."

"There are compromises one must make to succeed. I, too, have made many sacrifices."

173

Sandrine decided to play Irene's game for her own ends. "It would be a tempting offer even if I were not your prisoner."

"Then you will have no regrets when I dispose of your Marco Dante?"

"He is not *my* Marco. Our paths converged, and that is all."

"Good. I believe you. Now promise me this. When you return to your room, look at yourself in the mirror. You should take better care. You resemble a hag. You shall undergo another grooming. I cannot abide looking at unattractive people."

Sandrine narrowed her eyes. "Did you ever find Catherine Dastiel?"

"Yes, of course I did. I interrogated Catherine at Gestapo Headquarters in Paris. She revealed her excessive vanity. And indeed, she was a great beauty. A few slashes on her face made Catherine talk more than she had wanted. She withheld nothing from me. Then I arranged her escape from the Gestapo to Switzerland, which she believed was due to her own good fortune. I found a plastic surgeon in Zurich who worked miracles on her face. After Catherine healed, and again without her knowing, I facilitated her emigration to the USA."

Irene forced a nasty laugh. "I had a different face when I interrogated you. And so I arranged for you to be hired by Warwick at the University. Catherine Dastiel, I knew you wanted above all to claim your niece. I gambled you might lead me to her. I know how ruthless you can be. Did you not murder Michele's mother, father, and several more of your kin? I believe you may have disposed of your sister Madeleine too."

"It was a heart attack."

"Even so, your sister outsmarted you by making *Le Crâne* Michele's guardian. You could not challenge him in court because Michele would have accused you of murdering her parents. So, let us dispense with false identities. When we are alone, I shall call you Catherine, but for the time being, you are still Dr. Sandrine Arnoul to Warwick, MacAndrew, and the others."

CHAPTER 33
PARANORMALITY

Thursday afternoon, Michele came out of the shower feeling refreshed for the first time in captivity. No longer did she have to suffer injections and measurements of her body. Sandrine had been taken from her suite. Michele sensed she would not return. It did not matter if they observed her from an adjacent room. Comfortable in fresh blue pajamas, Michele lay on top of the bed pretending to sleep. Her captors had no idea how well the injections had been working. Although Michele's body showed no signs of maturing, she had already acquired certain powers as foretold by her Aunt Madeleine.

Michele placed herself into a trance and hovered out of body. Then she circled above the hexagon and monastery. Michele took in every square foot of the complex and its location relative to the main highway passing through Los Gatos. Somehow, she had to communicate what she saw to Marco. Michele had not tried it before, but she believed she had the power to summon her guardian at will.

***

After Conlon left, Dante went to his studio and tried to paint. Mié hooked her claws onto the bottom of his trouser leg and tried to drag him out of the room.

Dante disengaged Mié. "Okay, what are you trying to tell me?"

As if she understood, Mié led Dante to Michele's suite. Goji stood on the desk between the open book with strange glyphs and the brass bowl. Dante sat and stared at the writing. Nothing made sense.

Instead, water in the brass bowl churned. Dante wet his hands and moistened his temples the way he had observed Michele doing it. Mié meowed approval. Goji's eyes locked with his.

Dante floated out of his body and soared above the Peninsula. Michele greeted him over the monastery and the hexagon shaped building. Dante saw Sandrine below sitting on a bench beside a woman who resembled Cheryl Hale. He knew she was The Byzantine,

Michele took Dante through every room in the compound and afterward inside the monastery. Before they parted, he saw a helicopter.

"Marco, you must come for me me tonight. The Byzantine has decided to fly me to her villa in Turkey."

Dante came to full consciousness at Michele's desk where he held a pen above drawn detailed plans of the compound.

***

Dante met Conlon in a private dining room at *Bella*

THE SORCERESS AND THE SKULL

Venezia. Both had much to say. He let Doyle speak first.

Conlon brought information about the descendants of Constantine Theologos he found at the *San Francisco Chronicle's* morgue. He did not trust the *Times* because he saw the publisher at the Society of the Ten's gala. His research confirmed that Theologos' children and all but one granddaughter died violent deaths. Irene Theologos, the sole survivor, was suspected of eliminating every potential rival to take control of her grandfather's empire.: Constantine Theologos, who seemed intent on living forever; her father, the sole heir; three aunts; a stepmother; two half-brothers; even a husband and their two sons.

Many in the press and law enforcement believed Irene Theologos orchestrated the murders of the first Mrs. Randolph Clayton and two daughters. Within days of the funerals, she wed the widower, multi-millionaire entrepreneur and business associate of her grandfather, Randolph Clayton. In 1939, a pair of aggressive reporters exposed the Claytons as prominent financial Nazi sympathizers. That same day, both Irene and Randolph Clayton died in a fiery plane crash, incinerated beyond recognition.

Conlon continued, "That was the official story. No evidence of any heirs. No confirmation of who or what group controls Theologos' wealth and enterprises." Conlon concluded that when he reported to headquarters, the atmosphere in the department changed. The Deputy Chief of Missing Persons had not been seen for twenty-four hours. On a hunch, Conlon called the San Francisco branch of the FBI, ostensibly to speak with Agent Wark. He too disappeared. The same was true of the Police Commissioner.

Dante took his turn to speak. He described the paranormal tour he and Michele took above and through a hexagonal sanitarium and monastery in the hills south of Las Gatos. "I saw Sandrine speaking with a woman whose face and hair were identical to Cheryl Hale and Godfrey's nurse-receptionist. Michele showed me her suite, which was eerie, because her body was below us on top of a bed."

Conlon said nothing. Dante assumed Doyle was trying to understand the impossible. "Here's the proof." He reached into his artist's briefcase and showed Conlon the detailed plans he had drawn of the exterior and interiors of the entire compound. "We have to rescue Michele tonight."

"We will need more than you and me, and I can't count on anyone in the Department to join us."

"That has been taken care of."

***

At the *Galeria Serafino*, Dante, Conlon, Serafino, and Mazurek gathered at a table in the framing room. Rafe offered his hand to Doyle. "Sorry I injured your knee in our last game."

Conlon shook Mazurek's hand, and they exchanged brief masculine hugs. "My knee was shot anyway. When you landed on it with all your 265 pounds that was the coup de grace.

Serafino shared what his informants told him about the three men who interrogated Dante and obstructed Conlon's attempts to search for Michele. He had put a tail on the Deputy Chief of Missing Persons. This morning, the Chief picked up a police commissioner and an FBI honcho in a limo. They drove down the Peninsula past Los Gatos onto a side road south of the town leading to the hills. Serafino's men were too experienced to follow them further.

Dante covered the framing table with his drawings of the

compound. He did not explain how he obtained them, and Serafino did not ask.

"That hexagon building is a sanitarium and spa owned by Dr. Perry Godfrey. There is a helicopter here on the lawn that concerns me. They might take Michele away in it at any moment."

Serafino frowned at the drawings. "What's the security situation, Marco?"

"About the same as the White House or Fort Knox." Dante described seeing several two-men patrols armed with pistols and carbines walking around the barbed wire perimeters of the compound, and two more at a checkpoint on the road leading to the monastery.

Serafino promised to provide weapons and a crew of six. Conlon wrote on his notepad and tore away the paper. "We'll need other equipment too. Here's a list if you can supply it."

Serafino took it and nodded he could. "How much time before we leave?"

"Doyle and I agree it should be at dusk. That gives us a couple of hours to decide on a rendezvous point and how best to approach the compound."

Dante thought he heard Mié meowing in his ear and saw Goji in the window for an instant. Whether or not he had, an inspiration followed.

CHAPTER 34
INEVITABILITY

Late Thursday afternoon, attendants escorted Michele through an underground passageway to the former monastery furnished in a medieval style. She passed walls filled with weapons, freestanding medieval armor, pennants hanging from ceilings, and heavy furniture. They brought Michele into a luxurious suite in a private wing. After a long bubble bath, she tolerated a manicure and pedicure. A hairdresser trimmed and washed her gamine-styled hair.

Early evening, Michele stood in front of an ornate full-length, gold-framed mirror and liked her reflection. No longer in pajamas, Michele thought she looked older than her thirteen years in an elegant black velour dress with pearl necklace, matching earrings, and two-inch heels, her black shawl spread on a counterpane. .

Irene Theologos entered. Michele needed no introduction to know who she was. The woman's artificial face had the same plastic surgeon's signature as Sandrine's, despite having different features. Michele focused on her intense blue eyes and saw the Devil.

"You are a beautiful child. I admire your poise. I wish you were already as mature as you seem now."

Irene went on to tell Michele she intended to treat her as a favored daughter provided she cooperated. "How ironic, I have omnipotence without omniscience, whereas you have omniscience and nothing else. Our partnership shall be a perfect match."

Omniscience and nothing else? How little Irene knew about her.

For the time being, Michele listened without comment to Irene's schemes and dreams. The Byzantine had yet to learn how more she could now foresee.

***

Throughout late Thursday afternoon and into the evening, Sandrine went through a similar thorough sprucing, not in the former monastery but at the clinic spa. Afterward, an attendant brought her the gown and accessories she had worn to the Society of the Ten's gala. Sandrine dressed, and Warwick arrived wearing his tuxedo emblazoned with Israelite coats of-arms.

He escorted Sandrine across an expansive lawn toward the monastery. "You have become expendable, now that Irene Theologos has the girl. Yes, it shall be most interesting to watch how she disposes of you."

Sandrine ignored Warwick's gloating and preening. Then she became aware of an unnatural silence broken by Warwick's prattle and a coyote baying at an almost full moon. Sandrine noted the absence of security and floodlights. Something significant was taking place.

Warwick surprised Sandrine when he stopped half way

across the lawn. He revealed he was the leader of a conspiracy to murder Irene and take control of Michele tonight. His cabal included MacAndrew, Godfrey, Lusser, Astrid Lambert, and several other guests attending Irene's victory banquet. Why now? Lusser's serum had worked and accelerated Michele's gifts of second sight. Irene wanted to possess the girl for selfish purposes. The Society coveted Michele for a noble cause, to learn from her the identity of the Third Antichrist and the years the great battle between good and evil would be fought.

Next, Warwick recited a litany of slights and insults from Irene had had to bear without complaining. Sandrine had wondered how much longer Warwick could tolerate Irene's abuse.

After Warwick's further harangue about Revelations, Armageddon, and the Second Coming of Christ, Sandrine understood he had no choice but to include her in his conspiracy. She had unique value as an expert in all languages of the prophecies and the Old French Michele spoke.

Sandrine conceded she and Warwick had one thing in common. Hubris was in great supply this evening.

CHAPTER 35
RENDEZVOUS

Thursday night, a bright moon three days away from fullness on a cloudless night lit Milano Drive in the foothills south of Los Gatos. Headlights off, Conlon maneuvered his forest green four door '41 Buick sedan off the narrow road. A sharp bend led to a checkpoint a quarter mile ahead.

In the passenger seat, Dante glanced at his watch. Almost nine PM.

A 1942 black Packard 8 180 limousine arrived at the rendezvous point and parked behind them. Dante and Conlon stepped outside onto the road. Doors opened. Serafino and Mazurek led a trio of men toward them.

Conlon laughed when he recognized Serafino's crew. "Marco, they're all law enforcement,"

Serafino ground the stub of his cigar on the road. "Who were you expecting? Harry the Horse, Liver Lips Louie, Benny Southstreet? Inspector, I believe you know my crew."

Dante recognized two cops who worked off-duty security at *The Anxious Asp*, and Conlon introduced him to the third, a former classmate at the Police Academy.

Dressed in war surplus combat fatigues, the men blackened their faces and put on night vision glasses. They found the guardhouse deserted, and a bit beyond they counted a dozen expensive cars parked outside the monastery.

The men separated. Conlon and Mazurek moved toward the rear of the hexagon. Dante, with Serafino and his crew, moved through scrub and trees and over rough terrain to the compound perimeter. At an electrical wired fence protecting at least fifty yards of flat lawn, Dante checked his watch. Any moment now, Conlon and Mazurek would be cutting power.

Dante rasped into his transmitter, "Conlon, are you ready?"

"Electricity was cut by someone ahead of us. And Marco, you've got to see this."

***

Sandrine stood in line at a cornucopia-buffet of gourmet dishes and rare fine champagne in the former monastery's vast banquet hall. She saw no armed guards or servants. Irene served everyone at the buffet and thanked Drs. Warwick, Lusser, and Lambert for their invaluable contributions to the successful outcome they were celebrating. Sandrine recognized other guests she had seen at the Society of the Ten's gala who took their seats "below the salt."

Irene served Sandrine telling her she had lost too much weight. She filled her own plate and brought another to Michele, who sat at her right as if in a trance. Warwick helped Irene onto a high-back gilded and jeweled throne chair at the head of a twenty-foot-long table beneath one of three enormous crystal chandeliers hanging from sturdy ceiling beams.

Sandrine found her place card next to Michele. MacAndrew, yet to arrive, had a reserved chair next to her right. Warwick sat at Irene's left, Godfrey, Lusser, and Lambert farther down the table among the other guests.

Michele ignored Sandrine's attempts at conversation. Instead, she stared at her plate and invoked images of Dante, Goji, and Mié. Then she left her body and walked throughout the mysterious ancient city she had seen before, now empty of people. Loud voices and laughter returned her to the present.

Michele sustained an inscrutable mask concerned the slightest hint of a smile might cause Irene to ask questions she did not wish to answer. They must not know that Dante was near, very near, Goji too. Soon, all would be well.

***

Sandrine watched Warwick fidget and look toward the door every few seconds. Perspiration soaked his face. Obvious to Sandrine, Warwick was distressed MacAndrew had not come. So were other putative participants in his coup.

A series of tremors caused champagne to spill on the intricate woven tablecloth of gold thread and fine purplescent linen. Chandelier crystals shook and chimed. Irene Theologos raised her glass of champagne and commanded silence.

"My grandfather, the great Constantine Theologos, would have been proud of me and envious too, for I have completed what he set out to do. He instructed me well, how best to leave no evidence or witnesses. I have sealed the clinic and laboratory. Everyone inside is dead. I no longer need them. You all will agree that there must be no witnesses. That is why I have had explosives placed throughout the compound, and here at this monastery as well, all timed to go off after we depart."

Sandrine thought Irene planned well. No witnesses, she had said, which suited her own purposes as well.

"To success." Irene drank her champagne.

Excepting Michele and Sandrine, all repeated the Byzantine's toast and sipped champagne.

***

Dante ran across the lawn to link with Conlon and Mazurek at the rear of the hexagon. No guards patrolled the perimeter. Solid metal sealed the entire building. An eerie silence prevailed.

Serafino and his crew joined them. "The helicopter's pilot was on the lawn, shot dead. We disabled the engine anyway. What the hell is going on here, and what kind of building is this?"

The men stood in a group. No one had a workable idea how to break into the sealed clinic. Dante heard an ear-piercing sound more disagreeable than fingernails on a blackboard coming from one of the six sides. He motioned for the men to follow him. Metal on the side had been shredded like paper creating an opening. Dante scanned the area. No sign of Goji.

They entered the clinic. Silence and death greeted them. In a mess hall, bodies of guards and hospital staff covered the floor. Some had been shot; others, with foam around their mouths had been poisoned. One individual in a purple uniform held the military rank of colonel.

THE SORCERESS AND THE SKULL

Dante hurried to Michele's suite. No sign of her. In other private rooms, patients lay dead in their beds. Fresh needle marks indicated where lethal injections had been administered. Two women had faces identical to Cheryl Hale, one of them the suspended bandaged lady Dante saw earlier. All cursed when they entered a dormitory. Two dozen children lay dead on their cots. An adjacent refrigerated storage room contained shelves filled with preserved harvested organs.

"Michele isn't here. She has to be in the monastery."

***

Michele foresaw what was about to happen as each man and woman at the table took their first sip of champagne.

"*Crétins. Empoissoné avec grenouilles venins ... ici ... tout les homes, les femme ... tout morte.*"

Sandrine-Catherine understood what Michele said and dropped her glass. Warwick and all The Byzantine's minions from the Society of the Ten died instantly. Some collapsed face forward onto their plates. A few slumped in their chairs. Others fell to the floor.

Irene left her throne-chair and went to Michele. "So prescient, my child. Blue Frog venom is the quickest acting poison available I could find and adapt to my plans. And you, Catherine, your glass was not poisoned. As I said, I have need of you still."

Irene held Michele's hand as if intending never to let go. Another severe tremor shook the monastery's foundations. Chandeliers swayed in widening arcs. The room rolled and vibrated. Empty chairs overturned. Plates and glasses shattered. Poisoned victims tumbled off their chairs.

Michele stood and shook free of Irene. "*Vous, vous par*

Le Crâne seront defaits. You, you, *Le Crâne* has defeated you."

The door to the banquet hall burst off its hinges. Dante, Conlon, and Mazurek rushed into the room followed by Serafino and his crew. Sandrine-Catherine pulled Michele away from Irene and ducked with her under the table.

Dante froze when he recognized the redheaded woman.

Conlon pointed. "Look Marco. This explains everything."

Dante recognized the Deputy Chief of Missing Persons, FBI Agent Wark, and the Police Commissioner who interrogated him. Serafino led Mazurek and his men on a search throughout the monastery.

The banquet hall rocked again. Chandeliers and beams crashed onto the long table, and a mound of razor sharp crystal fell on the redheaded woman.

The quaking stopped. Silence prevailed.

"Doyle, can you see Michele?"

Conlon scanned the dead bodies. "No."

Michele crawled out from under the table calm and unruffled. "Here I am, Marco." She stood and clung to Dante.

Sandrine-Catherine joined them. Wild coils of hair took on a life of their own and enveloped the Winter Blonde's face. Dante thought she looked less like the beautiful Winter Blonde and resembled more the scrawny crone he saw for a mille-second in his last painting before it returned to its original state. .

He pointed at the head of the table covered by chandelier and ceiling debris. "Was that Cheryl Hale I saw?"

"No, she is Irene Theologos," Michele said. "The Byzantine."

"Theologos? The murderer of my mother's people?" Conlon tried to break through the rubble. "I can't get to her."

Serafino returned with Mazurek and his crew. "No one

alive anywhere in this monastery." He smiled when he saw Michele. "She's looking okay, Marco."

Michele tugged at Dante's sleeve. "Marco, everyone, we have to leave immediately. Irene planted explosives throughout the entire compound timed to go off any moment."

More aftershocks rattled the banquet hall. Dante carried Michele on the run to the cars followed by everyone. For an instant, he thought he saw Goji hovering above. Yes, it had to have been the chimera that shredded the opening for them to enter the hexagon.

When they reached the road, a prewar Packard Roadster sped past them.

Dante and Conlon spoke at the same time, "Sandrine."

Explosions shook the hillside, imploding both clinic and monastery. Geysers of flame from ignited underground gas lines split the night sky. Fire spread to surrounding brush and vegetation.

Conlon surveyed the area. "I'll stay here with my colleagues and brief the local authorities when they arrive."

"Let's get the hell out of here." Serafino slid behind the steering wheel of his limo and revved the engine. Mazurek took the front passenger seat. Dante and Michele sat in the back.

Serafino sped down the hill to the highway that would take them to the City. They heard sirens from fire trucks and police cars heading toward the monastery.

Michele had fallen asleep beside Dante. He vowed to do everything possible to make a normal life for her. Best he begin adoption procedures to make it more difficult for Sandrine-Catherine to claim Michele as a blood relation.

The Winter Blonde's radical change in so short a time reminded Dante of Dr. Monash's advice regarding

DONALD MICHAEL PLATT

Nostradamus and Time Theories.
    "That way lies madness."

CHAPTER 36
FRESH PHENOMENA

Michele pretended to sleep against Dante's shoulder during the drive back to the City. She did not want to be fussed over with concerns for her health and mental state. Instead, Michele savored the defeat and death of The Byzantine. Never again would that creature loom over her as a threat, nor her murderous Aunt Catherine, who had descended into a state of obsessive madness. Soon her life too would come to a miserable end.

Serafino and Mazurek cursed to let off steam over the atrocities they saw in the hexagon. The redheaded giant had been so anguished he vomited outside before he sat in the front passenger seat. Dante spoke of being reminded of villages in Sicily and Italy his army unit liberated after retreating SS units massacred every man, woman and child.

Michele sat straight as if awakened when Serafino parked in front of Dante's home. She thanked him and Mazurek for rescuing her and walked unassisted to the front door. When Dante opened it, Mié leaped into her arms, meowed a feline greeting, and purred.

Dante switched on the lights and asked Michele what he could do for her. She told him she was hungry but wanted to change clothes first.

In the kitchen, Dante prepared a salami and cheese platter with sourdough bread, mayo, and mustard for Michele. He brewed coffee and carried everything on a tray to his desk in the den. After Dante went to the bar and poured a stiff scotch on the rocks, he became aware how much his hands shook.

Dante sat in an armchair, lit his pipe, and asked himself if the madness that began with Madeleine Desaix almost two weeks ago was over and he could return to a normal routine of painting. Foolish question; his life had changed forever after he became Michele's guardian. Dante did not doubt she would exert a strong influence over his life beyond a sense of responsibility for her security and inspiring him to paint her portraits. It was something more, best understood as a mental and emotional connection. He had to face it head-on. Michele had brought him into a strange parallel world with creatures like Goji. Dante looked upward worrying how she might be reacting to the aftershock of having been held captive and the violent end to Irene Theologos and her accomplices.

***

When Michele entered her bedroom, she went to Goji atop the dresser. She kissed his head and thanked him for helping Marco at The Byzantine's compound. Goji stood a palm's width higher. Each of his malachite colors flashed the full spectrum of greens and further illuminated the room. They understood each other's thoughts in Goji's ancient language, and Michele experienced a conscious upwelling of new capabilities. On instinct, she sat at her desk in the library and opened the tome in which during trances she wrote strange glyphs. Now they made sense.

Michele removed the black dress and accessories. After showering, she studied her naked reflection in the full-length mirror. No physical changes yet, but despite her young age, she had control of her life.

Hunger intruded on Michele's thoughts. Not yet ready for bed, she put on jeans and a heavy burgundy wool sweater.

Dante was answering the phone when Michele came into the den. He listened for a few moments. "Michele, they want us to make our statements tomorrow at police headquarters. Think you'll be up to it?"

"Yes."

"Okay, Doyle, we'll be there at one."

Prophecy is History foretold
History is prophecy fulfilled.
Anonymous

PART IV

TRANSFORMATION

MARCH – NOVEMBER 1946

CHAPTER 37
A FULL DAY

Dante prepared well for the Friday interviews at SFPD Headquarters. Last night he phoned his father's former partners at their homes to arrange a morning appointment. He and Michele arrived at nine and gave separate accounts of what had happened at Irene Theologos' compound. Secretaries typed their statements and notarized them.

At one in the afternoon, they arrived at SFPD with the attorneys, handed in their statements, and went to separate rooms for interviews. The investigators grew uncomfortable when Dante mentioned names of victims connected to the Department he had recognized at the compound. They conferred for a brief moment and terminated the meeting. The same happened during Michele's questioning. Dante wanted to speak with Conlon, but his friend had been called to investigate a homicide in the Fillmore District.

Dante took Michele to a late lunch at *Bella Venezia* on Union near his home and introduced her to pizza. Raised to be a proper young lady, she resisted eating it with her fingers until he by example demonstrated it was the best way.

***

Back at home, Dante phoned Dr. Monash for a meeting. He was concerned about Michele's mental state. He told the psychiatrist what he knew about Michele's captivity and described the violent ending at the compound. She had not shown any signs of having gone through so severe an ordeal. Dante added he needed to talk to the psychiatrist. Monash told Dante he could see both on Wednesday of next week.

On his way to the studio with a mug of coffee, Dante saw Michele at her desk absorbed in old tomes. Goji stood sentinel at the edge near the brass bowl.

Mié followed Dante into the studio. He lit his pipe and drank coffee trying to ignore the cat's persistent meowing and scratching at the closet door.

Dante had an inspiration. He wanted to begin painting the first canvas for his *Black Swan Suite* and include Mié and Goji with Michele in the portrait. The cat increased the volume of her wailing and speed of scratching at the closet door. The distraction became intolerable. Dante touched the doorknob, which felt freezing cold, and twisted it open. An unnatural blast of icy, fetid air engulfed him. He kneeled before his painting still wet that should have dried.

Mié hissed and scurried behind Dante as if seeking protection. Had he feline hackles, they would have risen. . Being human, he recoiled at the transformation of his own painting.

Sandrine-Catherine's portrait with the snowy owls had been part of his Winter Blonde series. No brief change this time, the horrible transformation was permanent. Sandrine's coiled hair extended in all directions from her drawn lined

197

face. Luminous green eyes glowered with malignance. Dante's instincts told him he must destroy it.

***

Thursday night during the explosions at the compound, Catherine de Nostredame fled in a stolen Packard roadster. She drove to her apartment in Berkeley and found it ransacked, her clothing strewn about. She caught herself laughing. The quatrains Irene's agents found were altered forged copies. She had sequestered the originals in a safety deposit box at her bank.

Catherine got out of her formal and put on a skirt, blouse, and jacket. She found an oversized accessory, more bag than purse, and left the apartment.

Friday morning near her bank, Catherine abandoned the car. Minutes later, she sat alone in a room with a large safety deposit box. She emptied its contents into her oversize purse: twenty-five one thousand dollar bills; three different passports; a loaded .22 cal. pistol; jewelry; other documents, including driver's licenses, birth certificates, social security cards; and, most valuable of all, an envelope containing the original quatrains she had stolen the night of Michele's birth.

Catherine converted one of the thousand dollar bills into assorted manageable currency of less value, took a taxi to San Francisco, and went to a beauty parlor. She had her hair dyed brown and changed her makeup to conform to a photo in one of the passports, with a different identity, Sandra Arnell.

At a nearby used car dealer, Catherine paid several hundred dollars for a 1939 Plymouth, then found a furnished three-room apartment for lease in the Richmond District, on the corner of 26th Avenue and Fulton, across the street from

Golden Gate Park. She next took the signed lease to the nearest ration board and received a book of ration stamps.

At a Safeway Supermarket on Geary, Catherine bought enough groceries and toilet articles to last for a month. She purchased her favorite confectionary at *Awful Fresh MacFarlane,* dark chocolate raisin clusters, a case of imported first growths from a liquor store on the same side of the street, and a box of Benzedrine inhalers from a nearby drugstore.

Back in the apartment, Catherine put away her purchases and undressed. The mirror did not lie. She could not disguise her beauty and height with different makeup and dyed hair.

As night fell, Catherine laid out her fourteen quatrains on the dining room table and regretted she had not absconded with more. She wrote what she remembered of all phrases and words Michele had spoken under the influence of drugs.

Too exhausted to translate and interpret anything, Catherine was tempted to use her first Benzedrine inhaler. Instead, she opened a 1927 Lafitte Rothschild and obsessed over how, when, and where best to take Michele away from Dante, or locate the cache of unpublished prophecies.

CHAPTER 38
UNTIED LOOSE ENDS

Last day in March, 1946, Conlon arrived at Dante's home after ten PM without calling ahead. It was the first time they had seen and spoken to each other since the night they rescued Michele.

They settled in the den with their cognacs. Dante's home seemed to take on an aura of calm and tranquility, epitomized by Mié's insouciant cattitude on the mantel.

Conlon summarized everything that happened at SFPD relating to Michele's kidnaping and the immolations at Irene Theologos' compound. It was as if there were two Departments. One had a routine of the usual misdemeanors, felonies, and occasional homicides. The other held mysteries suggesting powerful outside political influences controlled the top brass and D.A.'s office without their knowing it. They closed the Theologos case. Statements by Dante and Michele disappeared. So did Conlon's detailed report. Top brass ordered him not to investigate who had taken control of Irene's empire. The official release to the press blamed a gas line for the explosion and fire at the compound.

The Joy McClellan files and shredding of Theologos' three henchmen disappeared. Conlon had no idea who silenced Mr. McClellan.

"Here's the kicker, Marco. I've been promoted to lieutenant."

"Congratulations, Doyle."

"Thanks, and how is Michele?"

"Better than expected. She has been going to bed early and sleeping well." Dante told Doyle Principal Stephens thought it best Michele not return to the classroom, which could disrupt the school and cause her more distress. Because he had recommended Michele for admission to Cal and Stanford, she could research at home and still earn a pro forma high school diploma. To satisfy the state and local bureaucrats, Dr. Monash wrote a medical excuse keeping Michele out of school because she needed time to recover emotionally from her ordeal.

Dante left Conlon to get some food from the kitchen but stopped when he reached the dining room. A tray of assorted cheeses, cold cuts, and sourdough rolls he had not seen before lay on the table with Michele's thank you note for Conlon.

***

The first week in April, Dante met with Monash regarding Michele's analysis. The psychiatrist had spoken at length with her over several sessions and concluded she was the most exceptional and baffling patient he had ever analyzed. On the surface, she appeared well adjusted, adult in both manner and conversation, a composed person with a strong sense of self.

Yet, much about Michele disturbed Monash. He was well aware of Lusser's experiments, which ended in death, deformity, or mental illness for his victims in the concentration camps. He could not say how or if the serum may have altered Michele's true nature for good or for ill.

To emphasize other concerns, Monash played recorded sections of their sessions. When he asked Michele how she felt about Dante becoming her guardian, she went into an instant trance. At that moment, something beyond static assaulted Monash's hearing until he turned off the recorder. He described what he experienced during Michele's trance. Unseen forces took control of his office. Walls and furniture undulated off angles, as if he were in a 1920s German Expressionist film.

Michele's case had taken him beyond psychiatry into the paranormal, the mystical, and the unknown far beyond his field of knowledge and expertise. He urged Dante to make an appointment as soon as possible to speak with Horatio Lefton. He had shared what he learned about Michele with the psychic who awaited Dante's call.

Dante stood. "Please phone Lefton and tell him I am on my way."

"In the meantime, be careful. Be exceedingly careful."

***

On his way to Lefton, Dante fretted over all Monash disclosed and what he heard on the recording. Michele's voice lacked emotion and affect. He became convinced the psychiatrist avoided using a specific word to conclude his analysis. Dante heard enough psych jargon in the hospitals to know what Monash chose not to divulge about Michele.

In Lefton's study, the psychic told Dante that Monash

had discussed Michele at length with him, coming close to ethical violations. Both accepted as fact Michele was a descendant of Nostradamus and might have the Seer's gifts of precognition. Monash believed she had an ability to travel through the fourth, fifth, and six dimensions of Time dreaming or in a self-induced trance. He had not mentioned that to Dante.

Lefton preferred to have a live sitting with Michele, but Dante thought she'd had enough probing from Monash and from Sandrine at the compound. He handed Lefton a piece of paper. Based on their previous meeting, he knew the psychic would want Michele's exact time and location of birth. It was the same as Nostradamus' nativity, which anyone could learn from published books about the Seer.

With the aid of an ephemeris, Lefton filled out Michele's chart with signs of the Zodiac commenting on each planet and constellation. Her horoscope diverged from that of Nostradamus because of different alignments.

Lefton closed his eyes rocking back and forth in his chair. After a few minutes passed, the well-groomed, natty psychic's forehead dripped with perspiration, color drained from his face, and his writing hand shook.

Eyes open, Lefton put Michele's horoscope in his desk drawer and locked it. Dante knew fear. He experienced it often in combat, smelled it from his fellow G.I.s, and now the stench of it emanated from Lefton. Before he could ask the psychic what he had seen in Michele's horoscope that terrified him, Lefton terminated the meeting and escorted Dante to the door.

"Be careful."

Monash's same advice.

***

First week in May, Michele stood naked facing the full-length bedroom mirror before dressing for the day, pleased about so many sudden physical changes. Her first period had arrived two weeks earlier, and with it, breasts had begun to develop, with more curvature around the hips. Body hair sprouted where none had been before. Lusser's serum had worked after all.

From the day of her rescue, Michele let her hair grow and experimented with mascara and different colors of lipstick. She laughed at herself for becoming no less vain than Aunt Catherine and Irene Theologos. More laughter. "And justifiably so," she told Goji and Mié watching from the dresser.

Aunt Madeleine had prepared her well for menses. She explained the necessities of female hygiene during that time of the month. Michele did not understand why the lady at the pharmacy blushed and whispered a response when she asked to purchase packages of Kotex and Modess, sanitary napkins as they were called, so she could choose the most comfortable.

Michele looked forward to shopping for new clothes to fit her changing body. Aching joints, called growing pains, added three more inches in height, and they had not stopped.

With puberty had come more visions, both day and night. What Michele saw and learned gave her confidence. Individuals and groups like her murderous Aunt Catherine, Irene Theologos and the Society of the Ten who wanted the unpublished prophecies, could never threaten her again.

Then, Michele saw a new menace in the mirror, not from any person or group that wanted to control her and possess the hidden unpublished prophecies. This was a threat to her freedom, perhaps her life.

She observed two men speaking to each other among a crowd in the *Galeria Serafino* during Marco's vernissage. One Michele recognized, Dr. Monash. The other she had not seen before, a fancy amiable man, but the more dangerous of the two.

"Goji, they want to separate us. I shall not allow it to happen."

***

Three AM, in a stained bathrobe that had been her clothing for the past month, Catherine replaced a light bulb for the table lamp. Foregoing food, she ignored the filth around her and inhaled more Benzedrine. She chain-smoked and drank strong black coffee. Obsessed, she read and reread each word of the fourteen quatrains she had stolen more than thirteen years earlier, the night of Michele's birth.

Frustration increased. One quatrain became useless because it implied The Byzantine's eventual defeat. Another described her part in a great struggle, but not the outcome.

> *La blond d'Hiver en fureur par rage de conflict*
> *Viendra a son le Crâne, conjurer non de dire;*
> *Que contre la jeune fille sera le plus grand afflict*
> *Et contre la foi elle voudra faire.*

> The Winter Blonde, furious in conflict,
> Will conspire in secret against the Skull,
> Wreaking great affliction against the young daughter,
> And she will break faith.

Catherine remembered Michele's cryptic drug-induced

mumblings at the compound, which she later added to her notes:

La Dame contra fille: Lady against daughter
La Dame contra Le Crâne: Lady against the Skull
Haine etre iceux: Hatred between them
Dissension horribles: Horrible discord

Catherine paused and thought about her missteps. She ought to have absconded with Michele, or followed her brother César to the secret location she had yet to discover. Filled with hubris, Catherine had been unaware how much Irene Theologos manipulated her life. Through Dante, she found Madeleine and Michele and watched her sister die of a heart attack. Next, something followed she never anticipated. Madeleine had made a complete stranger her niece's guardian and executor of the family estate.

Strong winds buffeted windows. Howling and whistling sounded through cracks, or was it Michele laughing across the City, taking control of her mind and turning it to mush?

Catherine inhaled more Benzedrine and chain lit another cigarette. Too late for her or anyone else to control Michele, she would use all her knowledge to achieve a different goal. She must discover the secret location of Nostradamus' unpublished prophecies before Michele found them.

CHAPTER 39
REFLECTIONS

The first week in June, Michele watched Dante apply the final brush strokes of the last portrait in his Black Swan suite. In the life-size painting with her arms outstretched, she appeared more nighthawk than swan. Dante had included both Goji and Mié, standing on top of prone, dead suitors at the bottom. Behind the black swan loomed her father, Rothbart, all in black, most of his face obscured by a hood, the exposed part illuminated by moonlight.

After Dante signed and dated the portrait at the bottom and on the verso, Michele pointed at Rothbart. "He resembles you."

Dante's reaction pleased Michele. He laughed at himself and agreed. A warm feeling came over Michele. They had become more attuned to each other. Marco, Goji, and Mié became her family, and she liked the routine of the past few months.

Michele had freedom to do as she wished and explored the City or spent time in libraries. She loved Golden Gate

207

Park and its domed Greenhouse, the Aquarium, the DeYoung and Steinhardt museums. Other days, she enjoyed Coit Tower, the Marina, and walks along the beach. Evenings, she interpreted the quatrains and read books on archaeology and biology she borrowed from libraries. Visions came more often and unexpected. Michele wanted to learn how to control them.

The Court granted Dante legal guardianship and estate executorship, which gave him control of her finances. He was generous with allowances and arranged charge accounts she could use at major department stores.

Michele chose Cal over Stanford. The commute to Berkeley was much easier than down the Peninsula to Palo Alto. Downtown, she caught the Key System Train, which went across the San Francisco Bay Bridge's lower deck and took her to University Avenue. A short bus ride brought her to the campus entrance at Sather Gate. Michele planned to take multiple majors in Archaeology, Anthropology, Biology, and Chemistry. Summer school registration would take place the last week in June, and classes began after the Fourth of July. Restricted to two courses, Michele chose to get basic requirements out of the way and took a Lit. course and U.S. History.

Before they left the studio, Dante surprised Michele with an offer of adoption. He believed a different last name might help obscure her identity. On instinct, Michele rejected his proposal without knowing why.

Michele told Dante she wanted to spend part of the day on the beach. In her bedroom, she selected a woolen turtleneck, gabardine slacks, and a USN Pea Coat she purchased at a war surplus store. She added Vaseline to her cheeks to prevent chapping from the bitter cold wind and put on a knit cap.

DONALD MICHAEL PLATT

At the beach, Michele walked past the Fun House at Playland with its roller coaster known as The Big Chute, a giant laughing woman above the entrance to its merry go round, bumper cars, distorting mirrors, and a spinning disk that threw off everyone who sat on it. She walked toward a less inhabited section of beach in front of the Sunset District and sat on the sand. She never went into the water. Signs warned of dangerous undertows that could pull waders out to sea.

For the first time, Michele wanted to know if Marco had been seeing any women before Aunt Madeleine found him, but she was not yet ready to ask. She did not think his face had been disfigured so horribly that no woman would find him attractive. After the inevitable success of his vernissage, she envisioned certain *femme fatales* clustering around him. No one had the ability to breach the protective wall she intended to erect around her Marco.

Michele immersed herself in the sounds of rough surf and the fresh smell of salt water. Moments later, she transcended time and distance and saw a vibrant city near Yonaguni on the southern coast of Japan filled with people, carvings, stairways, and domiciles constructed at perfect right angles. Somehow, Michele knew it had existed from eight to ten thousand years earlier. She watched, fascinated, when a tsunami submerged the city and cast its population out to sea. Many more lost civilizations yet to be discovered must be lying under water, sand, soil, and overgrowth with their secrets.

CHAPTER 40
DANTE'S VERNISSAGE

Thursday evening, July 11, 6 to 9 PM, floodlights pierced the evening sky in front of the *Galeria Serafino*. A cool jazz trio plus chanteuse from *The Anxious Asp* played riffs outside. A bouncer checked for invitations. Valets moved cars out of the way. Inside, Serafino, resplendent in silk tuxedo and gold accessories, greeted his by-invitation-only guests and handed each an elegant scarlet velour and gold embossed brochure containing Dante's biography and photos of his oils and graphics.

After helping Serafino greet the guests and hand out brochures, Michele stood near Marco's table in front of the Black Swan suite, watching him sketch personalized drawings on the versos of oils and graphics for a long line of customers. The vernissage had become the great success she had foreseen.

Michele had some minor triumphs of her own. Before they left the house, Dante complimented her as a stunning young woman who looked more mature and sophisticated than other girls the same age. Conlon, Serafino, and Mazurek praised Michele's beauty and agreed she looked grownup. Michele had reached a height of five-six. In high heels, she walked like a model in a one of a kind designer spaghetti-strap black dress purchased at *I. Magnin*'s adult section, accessorized with a pearl necklace and matching earrings from her family collection. A black and gold trim pillbox hat and partial veil completed her ensemble.

Well aware of appreciative stares from men and competitive scrutiny from women, Michele moved about the gallery and saw Conlon linger at the wall where oils and graphics hung from Dante's Winter Blonde suite. The inspector must be wondering where Aunt Catherine might be hiding.

Michele overheard people nearby praising Mazurek's frames almost as much as Marco's paintings and graphics. Serafino had promoted Rafe to gallery manager. The bearded redhead had on a rust colored fringed chamois tunic, matching trousers, beaded moccasins, oversized turquoise and silver rings, and Thunderbird pendant hanging from a neck chain.

Michele preferred Dante's more casual style He wore a mustard pinpoint corduroy jacket with leather patches on the elbows, forest green cashmere turtleneck, and dark brown sharkskin trousers over cordovan loafers.

One blight on the evening was the arrival of Dr. Monash with the renowned psychic Horatio Lefton. Michele resented their relentless observing and whispering to each other. Without any doubt, those two men augured ill. Michele tensed when Lefton approached the table with a Little Sorceress portrait. The psychic shook hands with Conlon and praised Dante. After introductions, Lefton asked Michele to sign the verso. She refused but gripped the psychic's soft hand. In a contest of wills, Michele created a barrier that blocked Lefton's attempts to read her. He began to perspire. After Michele released the psychic's wet hand, he rushed to Monash's side. Psychic and psychiatrist left the gallery in haste.

The vernissage ended at nine, and Serafino invited Dante, Michele, Conlon, and Mazurek to the gallery office for a celebration. He opened a more expensive bottle of champagne, poured a glass for Michele, and all drank to the success of Dante's maiden exhibit. Each of Dante's paintings had been sold, and most who purchased them wanted first refusal on his next pieces. Many oils sold beyond top dollar because rival collectors had bid against each other. Serafino lamented he should have priced the paintings much higher, the graphics too. Several out-of-town distributors and dealers had ordered more of them in large lots. Serafino anticipated positive newspaper and magazine coverage.

Michele sipped champagne with the men, delighted to be included, until a distressing vision appeared. She saw Lefton holding The Little Sorceress portrait, eyes closed, rocking back and forth.

Here was an immediate problem that vexed her. The psychic Lefton and the psychiatrist Monash would try to confine her and destroy Goji. That she had seen during her peregrinations in and out of the Fourth and Fifth dimensions of Time. Both men agreed she had sociopathic tendencies. Perhaps they were right.

CHAPTER 41
"... AND DUST TO DUST"

An adrenalin rush prevented Dante from sleeping, and he went to his studio. Mié followed, scratched the closet door, and meowed. Dante opened it and removed Sandrine-Catherine's covered portrait. He had not looked at it in over two months. Now he placed the painting on the easel curious to see what changes might have occurred. Dante removed the cloth and backed away. He switched on all lights to be certain his eyes were not playing tricks. Incredible, Dante could not recognize his own work even though the signature and date at the bottom had not changed.

Sandrine-Catherine, portrayed as an emaciated hag, sat at a table covered with books and papers. Dante could not tell if she was alive or dead. He resolved to destroy the painting but hesitated when the oils shifted and the image deteriorated to become a rotting corpse. Dante took hold of the canvas and felt intense heat before it disintegrated to ashes in his hands.

THE SORCERESS AND THE SKULL

***

The brass bowl shook. Water bubbled and whirlpooled. A candle flame flared on the desk. The Persian rug's rosettes and stars shaped for a moment into clear images of Aunt Catherine, and the water became mirror-still.

Michele exulted. *"La Blond d'Hiver... omnesque ... c'est fini. Elle qui a assassiné ma mère e mon père ... elle est morte, morte au dernier.* The Winter Blonde ... all ... it is finished. She who murdered my parents ... she is dead, dead at last."

***

Conlon arrived at an apartment building on the corner of 26th and Fulton in a foul mood. The phone rang as he settled in bed ready to sleep after a night of much celebrating and drinking at Dante's vernissage and afterward in *The Anxious Asp.* The same Deputy Coroner who had been at Madeleine Desaix's home the night she died had summoned him, promising he would not regret it.

Two precinct inspectors stood outside a second-floor unit holding handkerchiefs to their faces. So did Conlon when a powerful death stench enveloped him.

One of the inspectors brought Conlon up to speed. The manager had called the police because neighbors on the same floor complained about a foul odor emanating from that apartment. The tenant's name was Sandra Arnell, which Conlon thought sounded similar to Sandrine Arnoul. He did not believe Dante's Winter Blonde would use so similar a pseudonym.

Conlon entered the apartment and saw the DC wearing a

surgical mask. Crumbled papers, feces, and decaying food littered the floor. Conlon gaped horrified at what was left of Sandrine-Catherine rotting at a table covered with debris. He recognized quatrains set aside on a chair he had seen on Madeleine Desaix's desk the night she died. He took the quatrains as evidence. No need to tell the DC they had been stolen, and he would return them to the rightful owner. When he moved closer to Sandrine-Catherine, she flamed and disintegrated into a pile of ashes.

Conlon decided to wait until mid-morning to notify Dante and Michele. Let Marco savor the success of his exhibit, unburdened by another paranormal incident for at least one night.

CHAPTER 42
THE MEDUSA EFFECT

Michele greeted Conlon mid-morning after the vernissage and led him into the dining room where Dante was having breakfast. Conlon brought with him the latest newspapers and a manila envelope. He congratulated Dante for the success of his debut. Rave reviews filled the Society pages with photos of notables who had purchased Dante's paintings.

"Thanks, Doyle, I still cannot believe how well it went."

Michele beckoned Conlon to sit opposite Dante. She served him coffee and a hearty breakfast.

Conlon waited until Michele sat close to Dante. "What I have to say concerns you even more than Marco. After midnight, I was summoned to an apartment. Inside ...."

"My Aunt Catherine," Michele interrupted in a flat tone. "She went mad. Her corpse flamed and became ashes."

Conlon almost spat his coffee. "How could you know? Amend that. Of course you would."

216

Dante believed his Winter Blond portrait flamed at the same instant Sandrine-Catherine disintegrated. This he did not tell Doyle.

Conlon gave Michele the manila envelope containing quatrains he found at Sandrine-Catherine's apartment.

"Thank you, Doyle." Michele excused herself from the table.

"Marco, I see Mié watching us from the sideboard. Where is that green gargoyle? Every time I visit you, it disappears."

Dante let Doyle's speculations about Goji pass without comment.

"Marco, I must say Michele's transformation in so short a time is amazing. She is no typical thirteen-year-old. That is merely chronology. From a waifish child, within four months she has become an exceptional beautiful intelligent woman. Do you think Lusser's serum caused so radical a change in Michele, or would it have happened anyway? She does have a forceful personality too. Like you, I watched Lefton wither under her gaze when she gripped his hand."

Dante shrugged.

Conlon finished his coffee and stood. "I worry how far you will go to protect her."

Dante walked Conlon to the door and smiled to reassure his friend. "I suggest you look up *guardian* in Webster's Dictionary."

***

At 10 PM, persistent ringing of the phone interrupted Dante's painting session. Conlon was calling from Lefton's home and told him to hurry there.

Before leaving, Dante peered into Michele's suite. She

slept on her left side. Goji stood on a nightstand eyes closed. Mié lay curled against the small of Michele's back atop the blanket.

When he arrived at Lefton's home, Conlon, the Deputy Coroner, and Monash were conferring near the psychic's lifeless body. Other crime scene specialists searched the rooms for fingerprints and evidence.

Lefton sat rigid at his desk as if turned to stone. Again, Dante remembered seeing men frightened during combat. The psychic's open eyes and each line on his face had become a frozen mask of fear and horror. What had Lefton seen? Had it been something here in this room or in a vision? Dante saw no blood or any signs of a struggle.

"Heart attack, Doyle?"

"Maybe yes, maybe no. We won't know until after the autopsy. Dr. Monash found Lefton like this."

Conlon took Dante aside. "I regret I did not take Lefton seriously."

"I don't understand, Doyle."

"Lefton called me earlier this afternoon. He pleaded for a meeting and sounded so agitated I came right away. Lefton was in a state of absolute panic. He repeated the name *Medusa* but didn't explain what he meant. He was so terrified of Michele, he decided to sell his home and move to an undisclosed location. Monash had refused Lefton's demand to incarcerate Michele in an insane asylum, and he wanted me to arrest her before she murdered him."

"Michele is no murderer, Doyle. I can swear under oath she was home all day and evening. Michele was asleep when I left."

Dr. Monash joined them shaken over the sudden death of his good friend. "I found Horatio like this. He phoned two hours earlier in an agitated state. He said he discovered something about Michele that was beyond troubling. I rang the bell, but Horatio did not answer. I tried the door. It had been left unlocked. This was how I found him, too soon for so complete a rigor mortis."

The Deputy Coroner shook his head. "Not rigor mortis, Dr. Monash. Mr. Lefton is ossified, a most challenging anomaly."

Medics complained they could not straighten Lefton's body. They carried the corpse in his chair as is to the ambulance.

Conlon showed Dante a chart on Lefton's desk labeled Michele de Nostredame. Sheets of paper nearby contained notes and calculations, all gobbledygook to Conlon and Dante, with zodiacs, houses, moons and planets in ascendant and in retrograde. Mathematical formulas filled other pages, but Lefton had not written what it all meant.

"Marco, I have to ask. Has Michele been behaving strangely?"

Dante lowered his voice. ."I know what you are thinking, Doyle, and you are wrong. We both know whatever caused Lefton's death is not Goji's alleged MO. It is obvious to me, your friend Lefton frightened himself to death."

***

Dante returned home after one AM. He opened the door to Michele's dark bedroom suite. Thick drapes covered the windows. Light from the hallway allowed him to see Michele asleep, Goji in the same place on the nightstand, and Mié still atop of the blanket.

In Michele's adjoining library, Dante stared aghast at the fireplace mantel. A lifelike figure of a malignant creature stood rampant on the edge about six inches high, color of red soil, torso covered in golden clothes with jeweled accouterments of precise workmanship, all of an unfamiliar style. It was armed with a sword and a small dagger.

Dante touched the figurine's surface. It felt like marble. He left Michele's suite and closed the door. He had come to accept the vortex that continued to pull him into a world of unnatural occurrences and beings.

***

Michele had not been asleep. After Marco closed the door, she left her bed and lit a candle. In her library, she commanded the figurine on the mantel to disappear. "You did well with Lefton."

Seated at the desk, Michele opened her journal and wrote in ancient glyphs how Joy McClellan, The Byzantine, and *La Blond d'Hiver* had paid for their attempts to harm or control her. She dipped the feathered quill in ink and added Lefton to those names.

Michele reached into a drawer, removed a specific quatrain, and read its content. Goji's malachite colors glowed a gamut of greens, and Mié watched from the mantel. A surge of energy consumed Michele, and she reveled in the knowledge that all powers of The Understanding had come to her at last.

CHAPTER 43
SOMEWHERE IN TIME AND SPACE

Nostradamus was awake yet not awake when Michele arrived in his study, there, yet not there. He rose from the table and greeted her by the brass bowl on the tripod.

"My daughter, I have been awaiting you."

"And I have been seeking you."

Michele stroked Goji, inanimate on Nostradamus' desk.

"I see it has happened as I had foreseen. You now have The Understanding with knowledge and capabilities far beyond mine."

"Yes, I know."

"It will be a great burden."

"Be assured, father, I shall bear it well."

"You shall know past, present, and future."

"I shall distinguish each from the others."

"You may yet discover the secret of eternal life."

"If I do, I shall bear that burden as well."

"Use your powers to do no harm."

THE SORCERESS AND THE SKULL

"I so promise, unless I am threatened."

"As it should be. Now, come with me, my daughter."

They traveled back in Time. Michele wandered with Nostradamus through the library at Alexandria before it was destroyed, the Great Pyramid on the plain of Giza thousands of years before the pharaohs, beyond the Kingdoms of Sumer and Akkad, to a buried older civilization at Gobeckli Tepe in Anatolia, which she had visited before in her dreams and trances.

Nostradamus did not need to tell Michele the great age of the structures. She knew the identity of its inhabitants, the purpose of their massive buildings, and why the population and odd animals, some strange like Goji, disappeared.

"I can understand their writing. Is this the place where you found The Understanding?"

"No, Michele. You must travel farther back in Time to much older societies where you will learn about our beginning. You shall see the future in all dimensions. From this moment forward, you can wander at will without me in Time and Space. Soon, you shall be ready to read your best possible future, as I have written it for you, at the location of my unpublished quatrains."

After Michele awakened from her trance, she wrote in her journal all she had seen and learned. It included the knowledge of how she could communicate at will with Marco's receptive mind. Her subsequent travels in Time and Space would not be alone after all, but she would have to introduce Marco to the experience in short stages.

DONALD MICHAEL PLATT

Entr'acte
The Atavist

Why is it that *Prince Igor*,
Scheherazade and other works
evoking my lost Heartland,
arouse within me feelings
beyond esthetic pleasures?

The first notes are sounded
and I am in some Yesterland
that seems strangely familiar;

But I am no mere observer
of stock responses appearing
because of a composer's
Polovetsian proclivities.

I become an integral part
of some ancient drama,
its scenario implied
without full revelation.

The time is then,
The place is there.
The people are mine,
And I am home.

If this is the land
where my species originated
in some ancient epoch
claiming its lost son
through calculated stimuli.

THE SORCERESS AND THE SKULL

And if this is not the musings
of an overly romantic mind
in a properly pragmatic era,

Then I must face the bleak reality
That I am out of time
and out of place,
separated by the ages
from my race.

Donald Michael Platt

CHAPTER 44
ATAVISTIC STIMULI

Throughout the summer, Dante settled into a steady routine of painting. Each night, he dreamed of past civilizations unaware Michele was guiding him through Time and Space. Dante saw cities scattered around the world destroyed by tsunamis or submerged by instant rises in water levels. Others lay buried beneath ground the result of earthquakes and volcanic eruptions. Some had been abandoned because of drought and famine or overwhelmed by jungle growth. He traveled farther back to the apex of their days of glory tens of thousands of years earlier.

Those dreams haunted Dante and affected his painting. By September, he had created a series of oils depicting those cities. Dante applied gold leaf and shimmering foils suggesting emeralds, rubies, and sapphires to emphasize their wealth and sophistication. Strange glyphs and alphabets appeared on walls, tablets, and steles. Statues and bas-reliefs of extinct animals mingled with the familiar.

Conlon, Serafino, and Mazurek were awestricken by Dante's canvases of exotic cityscapes. The paintings had the

225

same effect on customers who visited the gallery, a feeling each had been there before, a sense of *déjà vu*, and a yearning for those lost civilizations. Dr. Monash described Dante's paintings as perfect stimuli to trigger atavistic memories through the collective unconscious. He purchased an oil of a majestic city buried somewhere in Soviet Central Asia.

Near the end of summer, Dante felt impelled to create several paintings of a former Ottoman Turkish palace he had not seen before. It lay on a grassy promontory above the Bosporus and the Black Sea. The oils portrayed the palace from different vistas. Each included a white canopy festooned with ribbons and flowers flowing in the wind above the sea.

No humans appeared on Dante's canvases until the last of the series. Michele in diaphanous white, floated above the lawn carrying a mixed bouquet of flowers toward an undefined male at the lower left corner.

***

Scratching from Michele's quill pen marked ancient glyphs on the parchment of her journal and broke the silence in her library. She described all she saw during daily ventures into the past and future.

Michele never returned to the University of California at Berkeley. College degrees held no value in any of her lives she foresaw. Michele discovered where Nostradamus secreted his unpublished prophecies and the biography of her future. The time was not yet right for her to journey there in body.

During her travels throughout different dimensions, Michele witnessed the origins of the Cro-Magnons and their extinction, interactions between Neanderthals, Homo Sapiens, and other humanoids. She discovered civilizations that thrived in the Pleistocene era, many of them advanced, all destroyed leaving none or few survivors.

The reasons why included great volcanoes erupting and shutting out the sky with enormous volumes of ash. Winters lasted for years and decades. One huge eruption lowered global temperatures to create an ice age continuing for a thousand years. Shifting of the Earth's axis and other natural disasters brought on drought and famine that eradicated subsequent civilizations.

More disappeared when asteroids, meteorites, or comets slammed into their habitats. Unexpected earthquakes, hurricanes, sudden flooding or rising sea levels altered geography. Animals were not spared either. An asteroid slammed into North America rendering many species extinct throughout the Western Hemisphere.

Great sophisticated cities disappeared below oceans and lakes. Michele saw where those lost civilizations' histories and advanced knowledge had been hidden or survived by chance. All that she must never reveal to anyone. In the future she alone would possess their knowledge and inventions, possess them all for her own use.

Michele traveled into the future and beyond to the Fifth and Sixth dimensions of Time, and as she did so, all other powers Nostradamus had described became hers alone to use.

During those same days and nights, Michele's preternatural powers grew and intensified. She did more than travel throughout the past. She journeyed into the alternative worlds of the Fifth Dimension.

Without having yet read what Nostradamus had written for her, Michele considered her two choices. She could become obscure and secretive about her powers or use them to benefit the world. Michele laughed at an irony when she chose her best option. She must become as the Byzantine, use her great wealth and power as necessity dictated. Irene Clayton Theologos unwittingly had shown her how to accomplish that, how to exploit cat's paws and useful idiots.

With new mature clarity, Michele understood she must acquire power over governments and political movements. How best to do that without becoming a ruthless tyrant?

Foreign born, she could never become President of the United States. Perhaps First Lady might be one path to take. One thing Michele learned from her U.S. History class and foresaw happening in the future: many First Ladies would select a mate each believed she could make President. Some mothers were no less aggressive when promoting their sons' careers.

Boys like Blake Townsend might be Presidential material, but that would last for a short eight years. Marco might be preferable as a spouse despite their age gap. When she turned twenty-one, he would be thirty-seven. That difference would not be a barrier.

Michele foresaw the coming decades of the immediate Fourth Dimensional future. Terrible times lay ahead with wars, genocide, regimes of vicious dictators, and horrors perpetrated on innocent populations. She saw worse, not better in alternate worlds of the Fifth Dimension.

Those journeys through Time and Space revealed to Michele her surprise free future. She found the best location to build a secret underground complex for medical research, and advanced technology taken from the past and future for her own use. It would be the nexus from which she could control governments. Had Nostradamus predicted the same for her or an alternative future?

A new threat loomed on the near horizon. Michele saw a coming age of machines, instant communication, and knowledge growing a million times added to each year by another million times. Some would use high-speed computers in futile attempts to decipher the meanings of Nostradamus' published prophecies. She laughed aloud at all their inevitable failures.

Nostradamus foresaw those computers and incorporated in his quatrains specific codes to confuse the results and cause machines to *crash*, as that terminology would be used in the future. A few would make money from their false results and be exposed as frauds.

So many choices to select. She lacked Nostradamus' experience to decide upon the best Fourth Dimensional route to follow.

Those travels in Time and Space convinced Michele that Marco knew the truth about her psyche and how she used Goji. It did not matter. He would protect her from Conlon. Although the inspector believed she commanded Goji to murder those who harmed or planned to harm her, no one would believe him.

Serafino and Mazurek adored her portraits and did not care what she may have done. Michele decided once she reached the age of twenty-one and gained control of her wealth, she would disappear from all except Marco.

Michele observed Marco's alternate lives had he not been wounded and married his fiancée. In each variation, she made him miserable, and they divorced. Afterward, he went from woman to woman never content. One alternate future made him happiest. She decided to ensure it would transpire.

Michele peered into the brass bowl as she did each night. The water rippled and parted. She saw the unexpected in the bottom of the bowl. Marco had created a series of canvases unlike any he painted before. Too self-absorbed, Michele had not visited his studio in many weeks.

***

Unaware of Michele's presence, Dante completed his suite of unique self-portraits. He did not know the source of his inspiration.

The last painting in the suite suggested a three-dimensional mosaic of malachite greens for Dante's face and background. If the viewer changed focus, a kaleidoscope of images appeared. They ranged from Dante's current skull visage to his original physiognomy. He replicated the same portrait in with foils simulating diamonds, rubies, sapphires, emeralds, copper, silver, and gold.

Michele studied Marco's dried self-portraits lined against the walls. If she stared at a painting long enough, she saw more than variations of Marco's face. Entire dramas took place as the mosaic of colors moved merged, separated, and came together again. Past and future emerged in the play of light on each canvas.

"Marco, they are magical." Michele peered deeper into the wet malachite oil he completed minutes earlier. Goji stirred on the table. Mié meowed from the couch. Its greens changed shapes, and Michele decided no one but she and Marco should view this particular painting.

CHAPTER 45
BAFFLEMENT

Mid-November, Michele accompanied Dante when he brought his self-portraits to the *Galeria Serafino*, except for the malachite oil she had taken to her room. Mazurek came from the back room where he had been completing the last two frames for Dante's Mysterious Cities suite. He phoned Serafino at *The Anxious Asp* and told him Marco had arrived with another series of paintings.

Dante showed them the golden self-portrait first. Serafino studied the painting from various distances. He compared its shimmering glitter to works by the Viennese fin de siècle artist Gustav Klimt. He gasped as Dante's face changed from the present to the past. Then he backed away.

"I can't believe it, Marco. First, I saw your face. Now I see mine, and ... *Holy Mother of God*, and now myself as a young man." He passed the canvas to Mazurek. "Look for yourself, Rafe."

Mazurek held the portrait. "Yeah, I see Marco's different faces, but not yours, Al. Wait, it's unbelievable. I see myself."

"I gotta' look at the others." Serafino stared into each of Dante's self-portraits and saw the same: first a variation of Marco's face, and then his. "Then anyone who looks at your self-portrait will see himself in these paintings. How did you accomplish it?" Dante shrugged, and Serafino asked Michele, "Did you have anything to do with it?"

"Except when I have posed for Marco, I am never in the studio when he paints."

Serafino did not hide his enthusiasm. "Marco, your self-portraits are even more mystical than those haunting cityscapes you created. We cannot put a sales price on them. Knowing our clients, we shall have an auction. Rafe, can you have these self-portraits framed before Marco's next exhibit?"

Mazurek sketched on a sheet of paper. "Conservative emerald cut frames painted in the colors of each painting would be best. Today is November 14. If I start working on them right away, I can guarantee they will be ready by Friday, December twentieth."

"That's cutting it close, but still in time for your exhibit, Marco. It's scheduled for Saturday, December 21. We'll have a viewing with champagne, canapés, and music, five to seven PM before the auction. Marco, you and I will set the reserves."

Michele observed and listened to Serafino's and Mazurek's reactions to Marco's self-portraits with an enigmatic smile.

CHAPTER 46
THE PORTAL

Unaware Michele had entered the studio, Marco stood deep in thought at his easel immersed in the painting he had completed minutes earlier. It was another oil for the Lost Cities suite, this one a forgotten civilization that had thrived tens of thousands years earlier.

Michele had visited its magnificent boulevards and buildings during her travels into the past. Marco had included the massive statue of its most honored citizen founder, a woman holding a scroll and a lamp. Michele had not seen the similarity before, but the Great Lady could have been her twin.

She sat on the sofa and stroked Mié until Dante became aware of her presence. "Marco, I have not seen Goji today. Have you?"

"No."

Michele went to her library. Still no sign of Goji. She studied Marco's unframed self-portrait of malachite greens. Michele had placed the six-foot high, four-foot wide canvas

233

against a bookshelf. It was much larger than his other paintings in that suite. She watched its colors merge and shift shapes, first becoming Marco's current and former face, and then hers.

The green colors mixed again but in slower motion. Michele's features changed until they became those of Goji. Moments later the chimera flew from the painting and took its place on her desk beside Mié.

Michele felt the thrill of a great discovery. No longer did she need to use the brass bowl. Marco had created a portal for her to travel at will through Time and Space whenever and wherever she desired.

Michele saw her chosen destination in the painting. She took a box of matches and walked through the kaleidoscope of greens, followed by Goji and Mié to a wooded area beyond a farm and tilled lands in the Provençal countryside. The year did not matter.

Unlike her previous forays into the past, future, and alternate dimensions, Michele was corporeal. She removed soil from a trap door, twisted the handle left and right until it clicked, and descended into an ancient, cold, gray catacomb.

Despite the darkness, Michele found her way to a vault. She lit candles on sconces, candelabras, and a centuries old oil lamp. They illuminated burgundy leather-bound volumes lining bookshelves with names of her father, mother, Aunts Madeleine and Catherine, and generations of Michele's ancestors. Gold letters glistened on the spine of the largest, Michele VII.

Michele brought her personal prophecies to a table and set it between Goji and Mié. With great care, she lifted the cover and read a dedication to her written by Nostradamus in an archaic scrawl.

Michele opened the next page of the massive tome and

smiled.

Quand le catacombe antique à lampe découverte,
Regner une jeune femelle ....

When the ancient catacomb with a lamp is discovered,
A young female shall reign ....

THE END

AUTHOR'S NOTES

The "unpublished quatrains" that appear in *The Sorceress and the Skull* are in truth fragments taken from Nostradamus' quatrains. The authoritative book about the Seer by Pierre Cadoux is fictional.

The author created all paintings by Marco Antonio Dante for story purposes.

ABOUT THE AUTHOR

DONALD MICHAEL PLATT

Donald Michael Platt is the author of five published novels, one book he ghosted, two books as a *with,* and a dark novel he is polishing as you read.

Donald was born and raised inside San Francisco. He graduated from Lowell High School and earned his B.A. in History at the University of California Berkeley. After two years in the Army, Donald attended graduate school at San Jose State, where he won a batch of literary awards in the annual SENATOR PHELAN LITERARY CONTEST.

Donald moved to southern California to begin his professional writing career. He sold to the TV series, MR. NOVAK, ghosted YOUR HAIR AND YOUR DIET for health food guru Dan Dale Alexander, and wrote for and with diverse producers, among them Harry Joe Brown, Sig Schlager, Albert J. Cohen, and Al Ruddy, plus Paul Stader

Sr., Hollywood fencing master, stuntman and stunt/2nd unit director.

In Hollywood, Donald taught Creative Writing and Advanced Placement European History at Fairfax High School where he was Social Studies Department Chairman for fifteen years.

After living in Florianópolis, Brazil, setting of his horror novel A GATHERING OF VULTURES, (pub. 2007 & 2011, finalist in the Indie Awards horror category 2013), he moved to Florida where he wrote as a with: VITAMIN ENRICHED, pub.1999, for Carl DeSantis, founder of Rexall Sundown Vitamins; and THE COUPLE'S DISEASE: Finding a Cure for Your Lost "Love" Life, pub. 2002, for Lawrence S. Hakim, MD, FACS, Head of Sexual Dysfunction Unit at the Cleveland Clinic.

Donald has four other novels published: his magnum opus historical novel, ROCAMORA. (2012 finalist for the International Book Awards}, set in 17th century Spain and Amsterdam during their Golden Ages, pub 2008, 2011; its sequel HOUSE OF ROCAMORA, pub. 2012; CLOSE TO THE SUN, A WWII novel about USAAF and Luftwaffe fighter aces and their women, pub. 2014 (3-time finalist in book awards contests); and BODO THE APOSTATE, pub. 2014, set in the 9th century during the breakup of the Carolingian Empire.

Currently, Donald resides in Winter Haven, Florida, where he is writing a sequel to HOUSE OF ROCAMORA.

IF YOU ENJOYED THIS BOOK
Please write a review.
This is important to the author and helps
to get the word out to others
Visit

PENMORE PRESS
www.penmorepress.com

All Penmore Press books are available directly through our website, amazon.com, Barnes and Noble and Nook, Sony Reader, Apple iTunes, Kobo books and via leading bookshops across the United States, Canada, the UK, Australia and Europe.

A Gathering of Vultures

Donald Michael Platt

Murder, mutilation, and carrion... in paradise?

"There shall the vultures also be gathered, every one with her mate." -ISAIAH 34:15

Professional ballroom dancers Terri and Rick Hamilton aspire to be world champions. Unfortunately, Terri's recurring back and health problems place that goal well out of reach. They travel to Terri's birthplace, Florianópolis, on the scenic island of Santa Catarina off the coast of Brazil to vacation and visit their best friends and mentors.

Along the picturesque beaches, dead penguins and eviscerated bodies wash up on the shores of paradise, and Antarctic blasts play counterpoint to the tropical storms that rock the island. The scenic wonder is home not only to urubús, a unique sub-species of the black vulture, but also to a clique of mysterious women who offer Terri perfect health and the promise of fame—at a terrible price.

Praise for "A Gathering of Vultures

PENMORE PRESS
www.penmorepress.com

ROCAMORA

DONALD MICHAEL PLATT

No man is closer to a woman than her confessor, not her father, not her brother, not her husband.

-Spanish saying

Vicente de Rocamora, the epitome of a young renaissance man in 17th century Spain, questions the goals of the Inquisition and the brutal means used by King Philip IV and the Roman Church to achieve them. Spain vows to eliminate the heretical influences attributed to Jews, Moors, and others who would taint the limpieza de sangre, purity of Spanish blood. At the insistence of his family, the handsome and charismatic Vicente enters the Dominican Order and is soon thrust into the scheming political hierarchy that rules Spain. As confessor to the king's sister, the Infanta Doña María, and assistant to Philip's chief minister, Olivares, Vicente ascends through the ranks and before long finds himself poised to attain not only the ambitious dreams of the Rocamora family but also—named Spain's Inquisitor General

PENMORE PRESS
www.penmorepress.com

HOUSE OF ROCAMORA

DONALD MICHAEL PLATT

A new life and a new name ...

House of Rocamora, a novel of the 17th century, continues the exceptional life of roguish Vicente de Rocamora, a former Dominican friar, confessor to the Infanta of Spain, and almost Inquisitor General. After Rocamora arrives in Amsterdam at age forty-two, asserts he is a Jew, and takes the name, "Isaac," he revels in the freedom to become whatever he chooses for the first time in his life. Rocamora makes new friends, both Christian and Jew, including scholars, men of power and, typically, the disreputable. He also acquires enemies in the Sephardic community who believe he is a spy for the Inquisition or resent him for having been a Dominican.

Praise for Rocamora, 2012 Finalist International Book Awards:

PENMORE PRESS
www.penmorepress.com

BODO
THE APOSTATE

DONALD MICHAEL PLATT

In a time of intolerance, following your conscience is a dangerous choice...

"In the meantime, a credible report caused all ecclesiastics of the Catholic Church to lament and weep."

-Prudentius of Troyes, Annales Bertiniani, anno 839

On Ascension Day May 22, 838, Bishop Bodo, chaplain, confessor, and favorite of both his kin, Emperor Louis the Pious, son of Charlemagne, and Empress Judith, caused the greatest scandal of the Carolingian Empire and the 9th century Roman Church.

Bodo, the novel, dramatizes the causes, motivations, and aftermath of Bodo's astonishing cause célèbre that took place during an age of superstitions, a confused Roman Church, heterodoxies, lingering paganism, broken oaths, rebellions, and dissolution of the Carolingian Empire.

PENMORE PRESS
www.penmorepress.com

Penmore Press

Challenging, Intriguing, Adventurous, Historical and Imaginative

www.penmorepress.com

CPSIA information can be obtained
at www.ICGtesting.com
Printed in the USA
BVOW04s1138111116
467347BV00009B/179/P